BRANDILYN
COLLINS

PLUMMET

Plummet

Published by Stonewater Books in partnership with Challow Press

Cover by Jim Armstrong
Author name logo by DogEared Design
Interior design by Steven W. Booth, Genius Book Services

ISBN 10: 0996961178
ISBN 13: 978-0-9969611-7-2

PRAISE FOR SEATBELT SUSPENSE® NOVELS
BY BRANDILYN COLLINS

"Perfect for fans for Stephen King."

—Library Journal, Vain Empires

"Heart-pounding suspense … an exciting, highly original plot."

—RT Book Reviews, Sidetracked

"A nail-biting thrill ride from start to finish."

—RT Book Reviews, Dark Justice

"Collins has written another taut, compelling tale of psychological suspense that weaves a twisty plot with threads of faith."

—Library Journal Starred Review, Double Blind

"Moves along briskly … the popular novelist's talent continues to flower."

—Publishers Weekly, Gone to Ground

"A taut, heartbreaking thriller … Collins is a fine writer who knows to both horrify readers and keep them turning pages."

—Publishers Weekly, Over the Edge

"Solidly constructed … a strong and immediately likeable protagonist … one of the Top 10 Inspirational Novels of 2010."

—Booklist, Deceit

"A hefty dose of action and suspense with a superb conclusion."

—RT Book Reviews, Exposure

"Intense. Engaging. Whiplash-inducing plot twists."

—Thrill Writer, Dark Pursuit

"A harrowing hostage drama."

—Library Journal, Amber Morn

Chelsea Adams Series

Eyes of Elisha
Dread Champion

Southern Contemporary

Bradleyville Series

Cast a Road Before Me
Color the Sidewalk for Me
Capture the Wind for Me

Dearing Family Series

That Dog Won't Hunt
Pitchin' a Fit

Non-Fiction

Getting Into Character:
Seven Secrets a Novelist Can Learn From Actors

WHY Did I Love (Hate) That Novel?

Any resemblance of characters in this novel to real people is mere coincidence.

Payton, Idaho, the setting for *Plummet*, is a fictional town in beautiful North Idaho. All surrounding towns and the area in general are real. The Kootenai County Sheriff's Office also exists, serving its county and citizens well. The characters in this story representing the county and Sheriff's Office are fictional.

In some instances, I have chosen to stay truer to my story than to the exacting processes of the Kootenai County Sheriff's Office. The fiction has to start somewhere.

TUESDAY, NOVEMBER 14

CHAPTER 1

'll tell you my story. I know you might not understand. But please believe I didn't mean to do any of this. Never in my wildest dreams did I think I'd be in this position. I'd give anything to turn back the clock. Start again. Be *me* again.

That first day it started I couldn't even cry—until hours later. The tears came cold and angry, full of revenge. By then it was too late.

It was Tuesday, November 14.

I hunched behind the sleek cherry wood desk I'd occupied for one week at Jack Larrett Financial, cell phone to my ear. My new boss, who'd insisted I call him J.L., was in his office, door closed. Forty minutes ago a brassy blonde, streaming indignation, had barged into the office, demanding to "see J.L. right *now*." She wore skin-tight jeans tucked into boots, a tight red sweater, and a white scarf around her neck. No coat, even though the temperature was in the mid-thirties. Idahoans know how to handle the cold. Since the woman and J.L. had disappeared into his office, I'd heard voices raised more than once. Good thing they were so intent on their conversation. My thirteen-year-old daughter was on my cell—her after school check-in call. She was crying. Again.

"Mom, I *can't* go there anymore."

It was her sixth day at Payton Middle School.

"I *hate* it. Everyone *hates* me. And I hate this stupid town and my *stupid* life!"

"Riley—"

"Do you know what Brittany said to me today?"

No telling. On Riley's first day at school a popular girl named Brittany Masters had raised her head like some hydra looking for a victim. My sweet Riley looked the part. Again.

"She told me I'm fat and ugly, and no one in the whole town of Payton will like me. *Ever.* And all her friends were around when she said that. They *laughed.*"

Oh, Riley. The words arrowed through me. What had I done to my daughter? She'd been bullied in Seattle, too, but at least she had a couple of friends. Here, she had nobody. I'd hoped and prayed this small town would provide a better life for her.

Riley heaved a sob. "Can't we just go back home?"

Tears filled my eyes. What home? Jeff, her father, had walked out on our marriage for another woman—after years of abuse to me. Now I couldn't even find him to pay child support. We couldn't *afford* to live in Seattle, especially with all the debt he'd run up on my credit card. And I had no one to turn to for help. My mother had died at sixty from cirrhosis of the liver. I hadn't talked to my father in years, I had no friends. Jeff had seen to that. Live with a controlling, jealous husband for long, and he'll scare away everyone else from your life.

Only a miracle had led me to this job in Payton, five hours away. Another miracle had enabled me to find a tiny two-bedroom house, barely affordable on my salary, given all my debt payments. "Riley." My voice caught. "I'm so sorry. Please hang on until I get home." I checked the wooden clock on the wall. Three-fifty. Another hour and ten minutes.

"And then what, Mom? What're you gonna do to change anything? I *hate* my life. I just want to die."

"*No.*" My throat ached. "Don't say that." Before we left Seattle I'd caught Riley with my bottle of sleeping pills in her hand. That shook me to the core. I'd thrown out the pills. But how to mend my daughter's heart? "Please just wait till I get home. Somehow we *will* fix it. You *will* find friends here. I know it's hard, making a change."

Riley sniffed.

"Do you hear me? Okay?" My voice clenched. *"Please."*

Silence.

"Riley?"

Fear for her wrapped around my lungs. Friends are everything to thirteen-year-old girls. Friends are the world. With them, life is good. Without them, worse yet, being bullied and shunned by others, life is intolerable. Hopeless, even. I knew this firsthand. I was thirteen once. And we've all heard it on the news in the past few years. Like that young, precious girl with so much potential who was bullied on Facebook—and ended up hanging herself in her bedroom. I have pictured that scene, the mother finding her body, too many times to count. It leaves me frozen in terror. It's beyond comprehension.

"*Riley*, talk to me!"

"Okay." The response sounded so small.

"Okay what?"

"I'll wait for you to get home."

I closed my eyes. "That's my girl."

She *was* my girl, all right, that was the problem. She'd learned her victimhood from watching her father beat me. I didn't know how to stand up for myself. Now I had to teach my daughter to be strong.

How to do that, when I hadn't learned it for myself?

It took another minute for Riley's crying to lessen. She sighed. "I'm gonna make some cookies."

I winced. Baking cookies was her way of self-soothing. But eating them only fed her weight—the very thing she was most teased about. It was a cycle I didn't know how to break. I could only hope this stage wouldn't last much longer. Riley wasn't really heavy. Just a little … pudgy. Baby fat, I'd say. I'd been that way, too, at thirteen. The weight fell off a year later.

We talked for another few minutes, until I was sure she was steady and I could let her go. "Riley, I love you so much. See you soon."

I clicked off the call and dropped my head in my hands. My heart broke for my daughter. Girls her age could be so cruel. Why did Brittany and her friends have to treat Riley like this? What had she ever done to them?

"God, please help."

The words slipped from my mouth of their own will. I shook my head. Why was I even praying? There was a time I had believed, after I left my parents' home at eighteen. I'd even asked Jesus to accept me as one of His own. Then I met Jeff, got married, and found myself right back in abuse. Little good my faith had done after that. During those terrible years, I still believed there was a God up there, but He had not saved me from the violence.

I know that may sound trite to you. The old *why didn't God help me?* question. Seems like we hear it every day. But it's not trite when you're the one facing it.

A female voice rose behind J.L.'s closed door. I straightened, listening, but couldn't make out any words.

I wiped the tears away, my thoughts still snagging on Riley. But the sounds pulled my attention.

Had J.L. made some bad investments, lost the woman's money? His reputation was stellar. He was Payton's most influential businessman and biggest civic supporter. Apparently he prepared taxes for just about everybody in town—and many in the surrounding towns as well. For many of his clients he also served as an investor. People thought he walked on water. And he'd been so kind to me, offering me this job when surely there were others more qualified. Offering me hope.

In J.L.'s office all went quiet.

Maybe this was personal. Was she his ex-wife? I knew J.L. was on his second marriage. They had a daughter Riley's age. She went to some private school in Hayden, just south of Payton.

I checked the clock again, picturing Riley alone in our little kitchen. An hour left until I could go home to her. By then it would be dark.

Work beckoned. I tried to focus but found myself studying the tall coat tree in the corner of my reception area. A long rugged pole of gnarled wood with deer antlers as hooks. Definitely an Idaho piece of furniture.

Would Riley ever be happy here? It was so different from Seattle.

I looked back to the work on my desk. This first month of my employment was a probation period. I had to prove I was worthy to keep around. If I lost this job, I'd have no savings to fall back on. Riley and I would be out on the streets.

A sound pulsed through my boss's door. My head jerked. What was that? Something ... muffled. I stilled, head cocked, but heard no more.

All the same, something inside me tingled.

I held my breath, listening, vaguely registering the gold plaque on my boss's door. *J.L. Larrett, CPA, ChFC*—Chartered Financial Consultant.

Still no sound. In fact, not even the low drone of voices.

Slowly I relaxed.

All right, Cara, fingers on keys.

I turned back to my computer, rolling my chair closer to the desk, and forced myself to refocus on my work. I still had a lot to learn. When J.L. discussed investment accounts with a client, he'd sit at the small conference table in his office, using a TV-sized monitor that hung on the wall. I would bring up the client's accounts, and all the information would appear on that monitor. J.L. could access the file with his own mouse, scrolling through as needed. I'd learned the task of locating computer files easily enough. But I was also responsible for paying bills, keeping his books, scheduling appointments, and generally running the office. With tax season coming up in January, I needed to send out tax preparation documents to each client. It seemed early to me, but J.L. said he wanted them mailed before the holiday season. In January and into February, clients would fill out their income and expense data on those forms and return them to J.L., giving him the information he needed to prepare their returns.

The clock read 4:10.

I laid my hand on the computer mouse—and heard J.L.'s door click. I looked up to see him in the threshold, the door halfway open. He was a large man, six-feet-two, with a belly. Nearing sixty. Bushy brows over hazel eyes. Thinning brown hair and a round face. He was wearing what he wore every day—cowboy boots, jeans and a button-down shirt. A gold Rolex was the only sign of his success. J.L. had a way of filling a room. He had a commanding voice and was charming and jovial in his confidence, quick with a smile.

He was not smiling now.

Something wasn't right. I felt it at the back of my neck.

I pasted a pleasant look on my face. "May I help you?"

He surveyed me, as if weighing what to say. "Please come inside."

"Certainly." I rose.

J.L. stepped back and nudged the office door wider. As I entered, he closed it behind me.

At first glimpse I didn't see his visitor.

J.L. stepped between me and the conference table. He spread his hands, a grim expression on his face. "I'm afraid our ... discussion didn't go so well."

I frowned. Glanced behind me toward the chair in front of his desk.

"She's over here." J.L. moved aside and pointed to the floor beyond the conference table.

I threw him a wide-eyed look and moved around the table to see.

In a horrifying second I took in the scene. The woman lay on her back, unmoving, elbows bent, hands resting on her shoulders. Booted feet askew. Mouth ajar, eyes open and glazed.

I gasped. Stumbled backward. "Is she ...?"

"Dead. I'm afraid so."

The word rattled around in my head.

"What *happened?*"

J.L. sighed. "She brought this on herself." He spoke so casually, as if commenting on the weather.

I gaped at him.

My gaze tore back to the woman. Her white scarf lay two feet away on the carpet. Red marks bruised her neck. Her fingers were spread against her shoulders—as if her hands had been near her throat, then fell away.

Realization punched me in the gut.

A forever second passed. I lifted my eyes to J.L., my head shaking back and forth, back and forth. A strange little sound spilled from my mouth.

He raised his arm toward me. I cringed.

"Don't be afraid. It's all right."

All right? Air wouldn't come to my lungs.

"I need your help, Cara."

He'd killed this woman? *Killed* her. Strangled her to death. And here I stood alone with him, his big body between me and the door.

"Are you listening to me?"

Who *was* this man? How could he do this?

"*Cara.*"

My gaze wobbled over the woman. Up to J.L.'s face.

"I'm sorry to bring you into this, but I have no choice. I need your help. And you are going to do exactly what I tell you."

No words would come.

"Understand?"

I stared at him, unfocused. "Why did you do this?"

"We're partners now, you and I." J.L. spoke calmly, as if to a frightened child. "We have to work together to get her out of here. If we both do our job, no one will ever know this happened."

My body went numb. "Out of here?"

"The body, Cara. We have to take care of it."

What? *No, no, no.*

"Just do what I say, and you'll soon be home with your daughter."

My veins went cold. Was that a threat?

J.L. pointed toward the chair facing his desk. "See her purse on the floor? Pick it up and bring it to the table."

My eyes filled with tears. *"Please."*

"*Get* it."

"I don't ... I can't—"

"Cara!" His calm melted away, sweat popping out on his forehead. "*Do* you understand what we're dealing with here? The trouble you could be in? You *have* to listen to me."

Me, in trouble?

Images stuttered through my head. Fighting my way out the door. Calling the police. I *had* to get home to Riley.

J.L. leapt around the table and grabbed my arm. I folded over, trying to make myself less of a target. It was all too familiar, a man's wrenching hand on me. Would he hit me next? Just one more violent man in my life.

What was *wrong* with me? Why did I keep inviting this?

"Do not *think* at this moment, Cara Westling." J.L.'s face thrust inches from mine, his words like dropped stones. "Concentrate on nothing but saving your life. You want your daughter to be without a father *and* a mother?"

No. *No!* This could not be happening.

I shook my head. The rest of me had gone numb.

He pushed me toward the desk. "Get the purse."

I know you'll judge me. You'll say to yourself—*I* would never do such a thing. That's the problem with judging—inserting your cool-headed rationality into someone else's chaos. Well, you aren't me. You haven't lived through what I have. You don't know what it's like to be stripped of your worth, to think you somehow deserve to be mistreated. To believe there's no way out.

Most of all, you weren't *there*.

On jellied legs, I moved.

CHAPTER 2

Riley measured butter and dropped it into the mixing bowl. Next came the white and brown sugar. No need to look at a recipe. She'd made chocolate chip cookies loads of times.

She couldn't stop crying. Every ten seconds she had to stop and wipe her eyes.

Why did her life have to be so bad? Especially this whole year. In January Dad had left—just walked out the door one night and didn't come back. He'd called once since then. *One time*. Had the nerve to say, "You know I love you." Yeah, right. Not as much as he loved Cindy Whatever-Her-Name-Was. And he'd told Riley Cindy was pregnant. Well, good luck with that. How long before Jeff Westling left *her* and her kid, too?

Riley added the vanilla and egg to the dough mixture.

Then things got even worse. Ten days ago Riley and her mom had moved to this dumb little town. Now Riley was five hours away from her Seattle friends, Kristy and Maya. Plus, there was mean girl Brittany at this new school. Why was she so awful? She and her little groupies. They were popular and skinny and pretty—and they knew it.

Riley hated them.

No way could she go to school tomorrow. She couldn't take their garbage anymore. After Dad left, Riley's mom started telling her she should never let a man treat her wrong. Well, what about other girls? Why should she put up with that?

Riley turned on the hand-held mixer.

The way those girls laughed at her every time she walked past them. Called her Miss Piggy. Her cheeks would get all hot, and she'd start to sweat. She wished she could just be a little ant and crawl down a crack somewhere. But it didn't stop at school. They put stuff on their Facebook pages about her, and on Snapchat. Oh, sure, that first morning at school they'd all let her be social media friends with them just so she could see what they started posting. And they exchanged phone numbers so they could text. By the afternoon, everything turned into a nightmare.

The dough was blended enough. Riley stopped the mixer and wiped her eyes again. Then dumped in the chocolate chips, hearing the crackle as they slid out of the bag. The dough and chocolate smelled creamy sweet.

If Mom made her go to school tomorrow, she wouldn't. Well, she'd pretend to. But as soon as Mom drove away, Riley would walk back home.

She pulled out the cookie sheet and dropped the dough on it, pushing it off a spoon with her finger. She stuck the pan into the oven and turned on the timer for nine minutes. Riley liked her cookies firm on the bottom and soft inside.

Now what?

She pulled out a chair and slumped into it. Put her elbows on the kitchen table and planted her face in her palms. Mom just didn't get it. She loved Riley and was the best mom ever. But she was forty. So old. She couldn't understand how it was, how Riley's insides shook. How sometimes she just wanted it all to end. You couldn't go through life with only a mom loving you. A mom didn't go to school with you. A mom didn't hear what people said about you all day, or see the faces they made. Little stuck-up snots.

Why did they do it?

The kitchen filled with the smell of baking cookies.

Riley hung her head and cried harder.

Her cell phone pinged.

She stilled. Her eyes moved to the phone over on the counter. It was lit up, but she couldn't read the text from where she sat. She stared at the phone. Could be Kristy or Maya from Seattle.

It could also be Brittany or one of her friends.

"Just wait till tonight," Brittany had sneered after the last bell at school.

"Why?" Riley could barely get the word out.

"You'll see."

And Brittany walked away with her best friend, laughing and laughing.

Riley had tried to push it out of her mind. Hadn't even told her mom that part when they talked on the phone.

But now she stared at her cell, her skin crawling.

Riley caught her top lip between her teeth—and pushed back her chair. She walked to the counter. The phone had gone dark.

Her heart started to beat hard.

She clicked the bottom button, and the phone lit up again. The text was on the screen. From Brittany.

FOUND THE PERFECT PICTURE OF U
MISS PIGGY. DIDN'T KNOW U COULD
LOOK SO GOOD. WILL PUT ON FB.

Riley froze.

A minute went by.

What would be on that picture? Something horrible. Something that would make the *whole school* laugh at her.

Riley let out a sob.

The aroma of cookies grew stronger.

The timer sounded. Like a zombie she walked to the oven and stopped the noise. She turned off the heat and used an oven pad to pull out the pan. Laid it on a trivet on the counter.

She didn't even want to eat the cookies anymore. Didn't want to do anything. She could only stare at her now-dark phone, imagining what was going to happen next. What the "picture" of her would be. Brittany had been planning this. She'd had time to mock up something terrible.

Riley eyed her phone again, knowing she should pick it up, check Facebook. But she was too scared to do it.

Not knowing was worse than knowing.

Wasn't it?

She wasn't even that big. Just not super skinny. At least her thighs didn't rub together when she walked. And sometimes she thought she was almost pretty. But her hair was nothing special, just dark brown and long. Her eyes were brown, too. Why couldn't she be blonde like her mom? And Riley's face was kind of ... full.

Didn't know u could look so good.

Riley thought of her mom's sleeping pills. How they'd been thrown away.

She couldn't stand the not knowing. People were probably out there laughing at her right now, and she didn't even know *why*.

Her nerves buzzed, and her arm felt like it weighed a ton. Riley took a deep breath—and picked up her phone.

CHAPTER 3

The mind does strange things in times of high trauma. Some moments of that afternoon are branded into my brain. Others are vague smears of memory.

As I picked up the dead woman's purse, my emotions leveled out, like water settling into rocks. Sheer action set in. A natural self-defense mechanism, I guess. Without it, I couldn't have done what I needed to do. For myself. For Riley.

I set the purse on the conference table.

J.L. managed a little smile. "See, that wasn't so hard. Sorry about grabbing your arm. That was most ungentlemanly of me."

My gaze returned to his victim.

"Open the purse." He spoke rapidly. "What do you see inside?"

I pulled back the zipper. "A wallet." My voice trembled. "Keys. Cell phone. A little bag, maybe for makeup."

J.L. leaned close to examine the contents. I could feel heat coming off him, could smell his fear. He wasn't as calm as he pretended.

"Move the wallet, see if there's anything below."

I did as I was told. Nothing.

My boss straightened. "Get her car keys."

I pulled them from the bag.

"Hold them up for me."

I obeyed. He peered at them, frowning. His gaze snagged on something. Acknowledgment flicked across his face.

"See that big house key?" He pointed to a large gold one. "Doesn't belong to her. Take it off the ring."

I tried three times before getting it off. My fingers kept slipping.

"Lay it on the table."

I put it down. J.L. hurried to his desk and pulled a tissue from its box. Wrapped it around the key and rubbed. Then dropped both items into his front pocket.

He moved to the office window, facing the street. The sun had set, twilight washing over the town. His back was to me, one hand on his hip, as he studied the scene.

I glanced toward the door. No way could I run through it, snatch up my own car keys and be out of the building in time. He'd be on me before I reached the hallway.

"You've seen the alley out back?" J.L. turned around.

"Yes." He owned the small building we were in. On both sides were other buildings much like this one. One housed a jewelry store, the other, a bakery. All the businesses had back doors that led to the narrow alley. Our back door was in the storage room.

"I see Paula's car out front." J.L. indicated over his shoulder. "Old blue Hyundai on the other side of the street."

Paula. Not the name of his ex-wife.

"I'll get her to the back door. You'll put her scarf over your head and around your neck. Take her purse. Get her car and go around the block. Bring it into the alley. We'll put her in the trunk."

The words nailed into me. This was *insane*. Besides, I wasn't as blonde as Paula, wasn't wearing a red sweater. Mine was blue. What if someone saw me driving her car?

No matter. Of course I wouldn't drive to the alley. I'd go straight to the police station. It couldn't be far away. I'd find it.

J.L. studied me. "You *will* come to the alley."

How did he read my thoughts like that?

Paula's keys weighted my hand. I could not look at her again, couldn't bear to see her mouth gaping. The dead of her eyes.

J.L. stepped toward me. "Do you know who my closest friend in town is?" His tone was low, the words tight. "Anthony Rainwell, Kootenai County Sheriff. He and I go way back. I know everybody in Payton. Who do *you* know?"

I swallowed.

J.L. jabbed his thick finger toward Paula's purse. "Whose fingerprints are on that purse, Cara? *Inside* it? How about those keys in your hand? I went to the bathroom, see. Came back and found you standing over her. You two had words when she walked in. You must have just *lost* it. I feel terrible about it. Poor Paula."

My mouth dried out. He'd done it all with such cunning. Made me pick up the purse. The keys. Words croaked out of me. "They'd never believe that."

"They'd never believe you." J.L. leaned close. "You want to go home tonight? Or to a jail cell?"

Jail? What would happen to Riley?

"Please, just let me *go*. I won't tell anyone. You know I won't, I need this job."

It was a lie, of course. How could I ever work for this man again? But I'd say anything to get home to my daughter.

"Cara, stop. You're going to do this."

"But I … I *can't*. I can't touch her body."

"You can. You will. Your daughter is the same age as mine, right? I'd do anything for my daughter. Wouldn't you?"

I was going to be sick.

J.L. straightened. "Get the car. Now. If you're not in the alley in two minutes, I'll call Tony Rainwell. Tell him what you've done. I don't *want* to do that, Cara. But I will."

Air clogged my throat. Obey, and I'd only get into this deeper. Refuse—and I knew he'd make the call. I didn't stand a chance against this legend of a man. The one who'd given a million dollars toward a new park in town, who rode up front in the Fourth of July parade and played Santa at Christmas. Oh, yes, I'd heard all the stories the day I moved to Payton.

J.L. walked to his desk and picked up the phone.

I pictured Riley alone as I was hauled off to jail. She'd end up in Child Protective Services for who knew how long, even if I could in the end prove my innocence. She was already so frail. It would be too much for her. She *would* try to kill herself.

"No, don't!" My hand shot up. "I—I'll go."

And I did, on feet detached from my body. First I snatched up the white scarf and stuck it on my head, wrapping the ends around my neck and over my shoulders to hang down my back. I draped it forward, hoping to hide some of my face. Then I snatched up Paula's purse and was out the door and through my front office. Into the hallway. Outside, the cold slapped me in the face. I kept my head down, crossing the street quickly. I remember getting into the car and throwing the purse into the passenger seat.

I drove around the block and into the alley. Deep within me a voice whispered it would still be okay. When I got home I would think through this. Figure out how to convince the police what had happened. I'd be out of a job. But Riley and I would be together. We'd flee this town and never look back.

In the darkening alley, I saw J.L. waiting for me, watching through the cracked open back door. I put the car in Park, fumbling for a latch to open the trunk. My pulse beat in my ears, and my hands shook. I leaned over, searching under the dash, left hand scrabbling. Where was it?

J.L. threw open the car door and pushed me aside. He bent down, feeling near the floor, then yanked. I heard the click of the trunk opening.

He drew back, practically pulling me from the car. "Hurry."

Paula lay just inside the opened door. J.L. shoved his hands beneath her armpits. "Get her legs."

No, no, no, my mind shouted, even as I grasped her leathered boots. Twice my fingers slid off; twice I had to grip harder, until my knuckles ached. For a small woman she was so heavy, the dead weight stretching my shoulders in their sockets. I managed to raise the lower half of her off the floor and backed out into the alley. The whoosh of blood in my head drowned out all other noise.

If anyone else stepped out their door right now, my world would end.

We reached the yawning trunk. I could not lift the body high enough to put her inside.

"Swing away from the car," J.L. demanded through clenched teeth.

I stumbled back, and he heaved Paula's shoulders and head into the trunk. He took hold of her knees and shoved the rest of her inside. Slammed the hood.

My ankles melted. I clung to the bumper to stay on my feet.

"Move!" J.L. propelled me to the driver's seat.

"What are you doing?" I fought to get away. "I'm not driving this car!"

"Yes you are."

"No I'm not!"

"Quiet!" He grabbed my wrists. "You want somebody to hear?" We both gulped air, our breaths intermingling.

"We're almost done, Cara. We have to get her away from here."

"You get her away."

"It'll take both of us. You drive this car. I'll follow in mine."

"I *can't*. I have to go home at five o'clock. Riley needs me."

"You'll just be a little late, that's all."

"I can't be late!" I couldn't bear to think of Riley, crying in our kitchen, wondering where I was.

"You *have* to do this."

I saw no way out. J.L. would not let me go now.

"At least let me get my cell phone." I could call Riley, let her know I'd be late.

"*No.* You cannot take your cell phone. Now get in." He pushed me into the seat.

"Listen." J.L. leaned down, speaking with intensity. "Turn right out of the alley. Keep going all the way up Third until it ends. Turn left, then right when you hit Highway 95. You'll be going north toward Sandpoint. Go up 95 out of town and turn right on Shelkins. After a mile it'll turn into a dirt road. Pull over to the side, turn off your lights and wait for me. Got it?"

I'd dropped into a nightmare. Any minute I'd wake up. "How do I know you'll come?"

His face contorted. "Why do you think I pulled you into this? I needed somebody else to drive the car. I'll be no more than a mile behind you. I'll drive you back. This will be over."

This would never be over.

"Cara." J.L.'s expression darkened. "*Do* you want to get home safe tonight?"

My head nodded.

"Then go!" He slammed the door.

My eyes closed. For a moment I hung there, weighing the rest of my life. Picturing the body in the trunk. This car would be like a neon sign driving out of town. Surely everyone would know—

J.L. pounded on the window.

I jumped.

"Go."

My hand rose. My fingers shifted the car. And I drove.

I couldn't feel my feet.

At the end of the alley I hesitated, peering in the rearview mirror. I could not see J.L. in the near darkness but knew he was there. If I turned left, he'd see. But he wouldn't be able to stop me. I'd drive around until I found the police station.

With a dead woman in the trunk.

And what would J.L. do? Call his best friend, the Sheriff. The police would be waiting for me by the time I walked into their building. I would not go home tonight. To Riley. I could not imagine what would happen to her.

Have you ever done the unthinkable for your child? Have you ever thought *how far you'd go* to save your son or daughter?

I turned right.

Following J.L.'s directions, I hit Highway 95 and turned north. Out of town I drove, pulling in puffs of air that could not fill my lungs. My body shook, even though heat was beginning to fill the car. One desperate name kept repeating in my head. *Riley, Riley, Riley.* Chaotic questions rumbled in my brain. What would I tell her when I got home? She'd start calling my cell if I wasn't there by five-fifteen. What would she think when I didn't answer? How could I walk in our door and act like nothing had happened? How could I sleep tonight? Or ever again?

At Shelkins I made another right, heading into the hills. After about a mile of narrow, twisting road, it turned into dirt. I pulled off the side and cut the lights. Anyone coming up the road would see me. They'd likely stop, ask if I needed help.

This was madness. I needed to turn around right now. Go to the police.

I waited.

The seconds ticked by, falling into eternity. They became one minute, then two.

Three.

Four.

I started to shiver. *Where* was J.L.?

Then it hit me. What if he'd lied? What if he never came?

My limbs turned to stone. I think my heart stopped beating.

But that's just what would happen. Of *course* he'd lied. He'd never come. That had been his plan all along. He'd sent me out here alone with a dead woman in the trunk. Driving her car.

How *stupid* was I?

The sickening thoughts ricocheted down the tunnel of my history. I'd been helpless against the abuse of my father. Then my husband. After all that, I'd had the audacity to hope. To think I was finally gaining a little strength. I'd found a new home, landed a good job after a mere telephone interview. Amazing feats for me. Now *this*. The most victimized, wrecking ball of a choice I had ever made.

J.L. Larrett—Mr. Town Saint and the County Sheriff's closest friend—had conned me into taking the fall for murder.

CHAPTER 4

Riley stared at her cell phone. Her hand was shaking. Even as a voice in her head yelled at her not to do it, she tapped the Facebook app and went to Brittany's page.

The picture was at the top of Brittany's updates. Riley's face, caught in a really stupid expression. Her eyes half closed, her mouth squinchy. When did they take that? Sometime today at school when she didn't know? But the body was worse. Her face was stuck on top of a pig, standing on its two hind legs. The legs were all brown and muddy. A caption above Riley's head read "Fat, ugly, and stupid. Three strikes—you're out."

Riley's skin went cold.

Her eyes dropped down to the comments. There were already seven. "Ha-ha" and "LOL," stuff like that.

A squeak came out of Riley's lips. She dropped the phone and slapped both hands over her mouth. What if somebody ever heard her do that? Now she *sounded* like a pig.

Riley bent over, arms hugging her waist, and sobbed. All of the past twelve months rushed over her. Everything with her dad, the time *he* called her fat, his leaving, and his girlfriend pregnant, and how he didn't want to be with Riley anymore but was fine having a *new* kid, and Mom crying all the time, and her getting the job here, and the move, and this horrible town, and the horrible school—*all of it* rolled over Riley in crazy big waves. The waves made her cold outside, and filled up her insides, until she couldn't cry long and hard enough. She heard her ugly sobs and hated herself for making the noise, but she *could not stop.*

Everybody would see that picture. Everybody. How could she go to school tomorrow? She *couldn't.* She wouldn't even get in the car with her mom. Didn't want to be seen on the sidewalk outside school. Some of Brittany's friends would probably follow her home, laughing and calling her names. Then they'd tell on her to the principal for ditching school.

Why were they doing this to her? *Why?*

She didn't want to live.

Riley's legs gave out. She slid to the kitchen floor and leaned against a cabinet, crying some more. She cried until her head pounded, and her face throbbed, and her eyes hurt so bad she could barely keep them open. Finally, all the tears in her dried up. She swayed to her feet and scooped her phone off the counter. Punched in her password and called her mom.

The phone rang. And rang. After five rings it went to voicemail. Riley smacked off the call.

"Where *are* you!"

She called again. Nothing. A third time. Nada. She screamed a message into the cell. "Mom, WHY AREN'T YOU ANSWERING?"

Riley ended the call and hugged the phone to her chest.

Out of nowhere, more tears came. She made her way to the table, fell into a chair, and bawled.

CHAPTER 5

I sat on the lonely road, mind spinning. What was I going to do now? Did I have any choice but to drive this woman's car back into town, to the police station?

Wild scenarios filled my head. Abandoning the car just outside of town, walking home. But someone was bound to see me. Besides, my purse and car and cell phone were still at the office. I'd have to go back there. What if J.L. had locked up the building, and I was stuck outside?

My stomach hurt. I was going to throw up. My fingers fumbled for the door handle—

I saw headlights in the rearview mirror.

I drew up straight, heart pounding. Was it J.L.? If it wasn't ….

The car drew closer, a dark SUV. Is that what J.L. drove? I'd never seen his car.

It pulled off the road and came to a stop behind me. I watched in the rearview mirror, unable to move.

The car's door opened, and the inside light came on. It was J.L.

Sickening relief flooded me. My shoulders slumped, and I dragged in a breath. Then a horrifying thought hit, the first of many like it to come. *Look* at me. A murderer had shown up, expecting my help in burying a body—and I was *glad*.

J.L. hurried to Paula's car and opened the driver's door. "Follow me."

He slammed the door shut and ran back to his car. Pulled out around me and started up the road.

I followed.

What else could I do?

The road twisted, full of potholes that bounced my already shaking body. After maybe another half mile, J.L. slowed and turned right onto an even smaller dirt lane. One with more ruts than the last. It had to be one of the service roads going into the Coeur d'Alene National Forest. I stayed close behind.

Darkness had gulped down the earth. And my soul.

My mind turned to a new fear, worse than all before it. J.L. would dump Paula's body out here somewhere, then kill me, too. Why should he keep me alive? I knew too much.

Riley. I *had* to get home safely to my daughter. That was all that mattered right now. Just get home. Then I would figure out what to do.

I saw only one way to get out of the situation safely—make myself invaluable to J.L. Convince him that he needed me and could trust me—not just for this task tonight, but tomorrow and the next day. I had to be his *friend*. I had no clue how to do that, and I shivered at the very thought. I'd never been cunning when it came to abusive men. I'd just been the victim. Now I had no choice.

The road snaked on, Paula's car bouncing. With each turn of the wheel I felt as though I ventured deeper into a cave, a spiritual eternity barren of light, from which I could not return.

In the heated car I sweated.

Finally, J.L. stopped. I stopped behind him.

Was I supposed to leave the headlights on or not? I watched for J.L.'s cue.

He opened his door, headlamps still shining, and walked toward me.

This was it. The beginning of my future. I pushed away all thought of morality and God's judgment—and focused on saving myself.

Something came over me at that moment, something hard and determined. I could do this.

Quickly, I unwound Paula's scarf from my head and threw it on the passenger seat. Reached down and pulled the trunk release on the floor. The trunk clicked open.

I got out of the car into the cold. "Where are we taking her?" My voice didn't even shake.

J.L. jabbed his finger to the right. "Through the trees about twenty feet, we'll come out to a small clearing. There's a drop-off."

"How do you know?"

"I hunt in these woods."

If he hunted here, others did too. "What if someone finds her?"

He pushed up the trunk. "Animals will find her before any human does."

A wrenching picture of the torn-apart body flashed in my brain. I shuddered.

"What do we do with her car? We shouldn't leave it here."

J.L. reached into the trunk and hauled out Paula's legs. They flopped over the side, one boot hitting the license plate. My stomach roiled.

I shoved the emotions aside. "Let me help."

Gritting my teeth, I slid my hands under the woman's knees. J.L. took hold of her shoulders, and together we heaved her out.

"This way." J.L. started backing into the trees, looking over his shoulder. The headlights of the two cars gave us penumbral light. I staggered behind him, breathing the frigid air and telling myself to stay strong. Focused. We wove around trees and stumbled over bushes, the light growing dimmer until it was nearly gone. My arms were about to give out when we shuffled into the clearing. J.L. halted.

"Put her down."

Paula's body thumped to the ground.

"The cliff's right here." J.L. pointed a few feet from where he stood.

My eyes could barely see it in the dark. "How far down?"

"Fifty feet, maybe."

Enough to break my neck if he threw me over.

Fresh fear took hold of me, raw, mind-numbing fear. I pictured Riley in our house, calling me, wondering where I was. She *needed* me. I would not leave her alone. I would not let her go through life without a mother.

"*What* are we going to do with her car, J.L.?"

"You're going to drive it where I tell you."

My insides unwound. The relief would have dropped me to my knees if I'd let it. He wasn't going to leave me there after all. He had further work for me.

But new anxiety gripped me. I'd be driving Paula's car again. More chances of someone seeing me.

I'd put her scarf back on. Stay on the outskirts of town.

Such schemes in my head. How long ago was it that J.L. had called me into his office? An hour? How had I descended to *this* in such a short time?

J.L. wiped his forehead with his sleeve. "Step back."

I obeyed.

He moved behind Paula's body and tugged her around until she was parallel with the cliff. Then he rolled her forward—until she disappeared.

I listened, trembling, to the sound of her body's crashing.

Silence.

Paula was gone. Just like that. A person wiped from the face of the earth.

I sucked in a breath. My hands were so cold I could hardly feel them.

J.L. straightened. "I'm sorry, Cara. Really."

I couldn't think of a response.

"All right." He sighed. "Let's go."

I made my way ahead of him back through the darkness to the growing light of the cars.

"Wait," J.L. said when we reached the road, "I have gloves for you." He retrieved them off the passenger seat of his SUV—work gloves large enough for a man. He also brought back a small towel. "Put these on." He shoved the gloves in my hand. "Get in and use the scarf to wipe down everywhere inside the car that you've touched. I'll take care of the outside and the trunk. You also need to wipe the purse and everything in it, including her cell phone."

Fingerprints. Of course. He'd thought of everything.

Had he done this before?

"What about the car? Where are we taking it?"

"Back closer to 95."

"Someone will find it. Soon."

"Doesn't matter. It'll look like she abandoned it. Just follow me. When we stop, take the keys out of the ignition. Clean them off and put them in her purse. Bring the purse and scarf with you. I'll get rid of them." He pointed at me. "*Don't* miss anything when you wipe down. Do that now."

He opened the car door, and I slid in, turning on the overhead light. J.L. closed the door and wiped it down with his towel. I picked up the scarf and went to work on the steering wheel, the dashboard, inside the door, the console. My hands were clumsy in the large gloves. When I thought I was done, I went over everything again. One small slip—and I was doomed. Then I started on the purse, taking out everything it held piece by piece, and going over the handbag itself, inside and out.

Only then did it occur me—the car and purse would be *too* clean. Paula's prints should be all over them. I stilled. We should have saved Paula's body until after we cleaned the car. Used her fingers to—

I squeezed my eyes shut.

J.L. thumped the window, towel in hand. "You done?" His voice muffled through the glass.

"Yes."

He headed to his car.

On the narrow road J.L. needed a number of back-and-forth maneuvers to get his car pointed in the other direction. He waited for me as I turned around.

We drove out, my body bouncing and mind racing. What had I forgotten to wipe off? Had J.L. gotten all the prints off the trunk? What if a print of his was found? Would he be able to explain it away? He'd made it sound as if the police would never suspect him,

even with evidence staring them in the face. But one of *my* prints
….

We drove on. Back to civilization, back to my life as it had now become. We left the service road, turning onto the dirt lane that would eventually lead to pavement. After that my mind lost all logical thought, everything jumbling in my head.

J.L. pulled into a dirt clearing on the right. I followed.

I turned off the engine with my gloved hand, yanked out the keys and wiped them off. Dropped them into Paula's purse. I snatched up the purse and scarf and slid out of the car. Then froze. What had I missed? Tonight when I tried to sleep, I knew I'd think of something. Tomorrow and forever, I would look back to this moment and wish I'd realized it in time. That *something* would haunt me, fill me with the terrible knowledge that one day the police would come knocking on my door—

"Cara!" J.L. called through his opened window. "Come *on!*"

I slammed Paula's car door and ran to J.L.'s vehicle. Got in. Threw the purse and scarf on the floor.

"You have the keys?" J.L.'s words flew at me.

"In her purse."

"Cell phone's there too?"

I nodded.

"Everything wiped down? *Everything.*"

I hesitated. "Yes."

"Good, Cara. Good. Keep the gloves on and pull out her cell phone. We need to remove the battery if we can."

I took the phone from Paula's handbag. J.L. shone a flashlight from his own cell so we could see what we were doing. Paula's was an older model iPhone, one that had a removable battery. But I couldn't get my fingers to work in the clumsy gloves. J.L. handed his cell to me and ended up taking Paula's phone in his bare hands to remove its battery. When he was done he wiped the phone and battery clean of prints and dropped them back in her purse.

My heart ground out beats. Every second seemed so long. What if someone drove by? "Where can we get rid of this?" I pointed a trembling finger at the purse.

J.L. didn't answer. He shoved the car into Drive and pulled onto the road.

We drove on through the darkness, leaving Paula's rubbed down car that surely, *surely* held a spot of evidence somewhere. A spot that would send me to prison and leave my daughter alone.

CHAPTER 6

When we hit Highway 95, J.L. turned south toward Payton. He didn't stay on 95 long, soon veering onto a side street. I still wore the gloves, no energy to take them off.

My pulse had slowed. Now my heart didn't want to beat at all. I felt … dead. Emptiness glazed over.

My eyes fell on the dashboard clock. Five-thirty. I would be late getting home to Riley. She must be so worried.

One hour and twenty minutes ago my life had been normal. At least *my* normal. Look at what I had become.

Why had this happened?

"Who was she?" I turned to look at J.L.'s profile. "Paula who?"

He sighed. "Tellinger."

"A client?"

"No. She lived in Payton with a man who's a client. They had a bad break-up."

"Why was she so mad at you?"

J.L.'s mouth pulled down. "She was taking their break-up out on me."

I stared at him. "*That* was reason to kill her?"

He threw me a glance. "She'd have brought me down, Cara. She threatened me. She threatened my *family*." J.L. shook his head. "Do what you want to me. But nobody threatens my wife and daughter."

I thought of my ex-husband's abuse. How he could beat up on me. But if he'd ever touched my girl …

"Look." J.L. drew a hand across his face. "We're a team now. You helped me out of a bad mess. It's done, and we can forget about it. But I won't forget what you did for me. I'm loyal to my friends. I'm here for you, completely. Anything you need, just let me know."

My hands were getting hot. I pulled off the gloves and stared at my fingers, remembering what they'd done. A new wave of panic washed over me. "The police will come asking, don't you think? She'll be missing. Somebody must know she came to the office. We'll be the last people who saw her."

"Not police. Payton contracts with the Kootenai County Sheriff's Office."

The news stunned me. Imagine if I'd disobeyed J.L. and tried to find the town's police station. I'd still be looking. And no wonder he'd mentioned the Sheriff was his best friend.

It took me a moment to find my tongue. "Well, whoever. Some deputy, then. They'll come."

"I'll deal with them. They won't be a problem."

"But they'll ask. What if they ask *me?* What am I supposed to say?"

"That she came. She was angry. She went into my office, and I closed the door. We talked and she left at ... What time did you go out to her car?"

I double checked the timeframe in my mind. "You came out of your office around 4:15. So I left around 4:30."

"Okay. Paula left around 4:30. She had her white scarf wrapped around her head. That's all you know."

It couldn't be that easy. "What if someone saw her come, then saw her—*me*—leave? She was wearing a red sweater. Mine is blue."

"People won't think that much about it. 'Was her sweater red or blue? I can't remember.' Before long someone will find her car. It'll look strange, abandoned on a rural road. But Paula and Vince—the guy she lived with—don't exactly run with a great crowd. They're people on the fringes, despite the fact that he owns a successful construction company. The Sheriff's Office knows that. Deputies have been called out to their place more than once on domestic issues."

I pressed back in the seat. "Are we supposed to let them think *he* did it?" I couldn't live with that—sending an innocent man to jail.

"Vince can take care of himself."

I didn't care to pursue what that might mean.

We were on residential streets, not far from downtown Payton. Someone might see J.L. and me driving together. His car, our profiles, lit by the spill of a streetlight. A casual glance that later would become hugely important in court ...

"What about security cameras?" I asked. "Near businesses and at stop lights?"

"That's why I had you put her scarf over your head. Also, it was getting dark, and those films are always grainy. They'll think you were her. They'll think she met up with someone off the main road. Took off with that person. Her life with Vince is over, what's the point of staying here?"

"We have to get rid of this purse." The thing felt like a time bomb sitting at my feet.

"I will."

"Some place where it won't ever be found." My voice rose. "We have to do it now!"

"Cara. I'll take care of it."

But what if he didn't? What if he made a mistake?

My thoughts raced on. "What about phone tracking? We took her cell into the forest."

"We went too far in. There's no service back there. You have got to calm down."

My brain thrashed for something, *anything* we'd missed. "What about cameras in the alley? They'd have us on film, putting her body in the trunk!" That realization seized up my lungs. "You have to get the film—"

"There *aren't* any cameras back there. Stop now, Cara. We'll be fine. You have to believe that. And if any deputy tries to question you at home or bothers you, just come to me. I'll deal with it."

J.L. just wanted to keep me close so he'd know what I was doing. How could I ever get away from this man? If I quit my job, he'd view my leaving as a threat. He wouldn't *let* me go.

We drove down Eighth to Corbin, the main street in Payton, and turned right. J.L.'s building was in the 300 block. He turned right onto Fourth Street, then left into the alley and parked by our back entrance.

"Let's get inside. Hurry." He opened his door.

"When are you going to take care of the purse? And her scarf?"

"Cara. Come on."

I stumbled after him into the building.

In our front office, I stilled, my body going weak. All the energy I'd summoned drained out my feet. My eyes fixed on my desk. Same chair, same computer. My spot. Two hours ago they'd represented my new life, fighting out of victimhood.

What was I supposed to do now, in this new, uncharted territory? I'd be better back with Jeff, feeling the smack of his fist.

"Cara." J.L. touched my arm. I flinched, and he pulled away, palms out—*I'm sorry.* "Everything will be fine. Trust me. And remember, you need me for anything, I'll make it happen."

How about erasing the last hour and a half?

"You hear me?"

"Yes."

"Good. Now go home to your daughter."

Riley. Resolve trickled into my veins.

I picked up my cell and tapped in the password. Riley had phoned five times, three of the calls even before I should have gotten home. That wasn't like her. What had happened? While I was getting rid of a body, *what* had happened to my daughter?

I grabbed my purse and coat and ran out the door.

CHAPTER 7

As I hustled to my car, fueled by fresh panic, I punched in Riley's number, not stopping to listen to her message. She answered on the first ring.

"Where have you *been?*" The last word ended with a sob.

"I'm so sorry, I was busy and not near my phone. What happened?"

"Brittany put a picture of me on Facebook! And everybody's seeing it and commenting and calling me names. I *hate* it here. I'm *never* going back to that school!"

Anger sprayed through me. I reached the car and yanked the door open. How *could* that nasty girl do this to my daughter? Look what I'd just gone through—for her sake. Now some thirteen-year-old girl was playing with Riley's life?

"Listen." I fought to keep my tone calm. "I'm on my way home. We'll talk, okay? I'll be there in five minutes."

A moment passed before she responded. "Please just get here."

I threw my things on my passenger seat and started my old Subaru. Not until then did I notice the cold. I hadn't stopped to put on my coat.

On the short drive home memories bombarded me. Paula. The dirt road. Her body flopped into the trunk. Crashing over the cliff. I thrust them all aside. I had to be strong. Comfort Riley. And somehow stop a bully while not becoming one myself. Which is what I would look like to my daughter—forcing her to return to a school that housed a pit of vipers.

I pulled into the garage of our little house on Grant Street and shut off the engine. Hit the remote button to close the door. Leaving everything in the car, I hurried through the door into the back area that housed the washer and dryer. "Riley?" I strode into the kitchen.

"Mommmm." She threw herself into my arms and sobbed.

"Oh, honey."

I urged her into the living area and down onto our threadbare couch. What to do then but hold her and let her cry? I stroked her hair, murmuring, "It'll be okay" and "We'll get through this." Platitudes. How well I remembered what it was like to be thirteen and lonely. And I knew the desperation of feeling helpless in the face of cruelty.

In the past few hours I'd allowed myself to be victimized *again*. After I'd vowed to rebuild my life. I was a failure, but my daughter had a chance. She could break the cycle.

When Riley's tears ran out, I fetched a box of tissues and pushed one into her fist. "Now." I brushed away strands of hair stuck to her cheek. "I want you to tell me exactly what happened. And show me what's on Facebook."

It was worse than I'd expected.

I stared at the contemptuous picture on Riley's phone, my mouth pinched and fingers curled. A mock-up photo of a pig and my sweet daughter's face. My feet pressed hard against the floor, steadying my body. I wanted to hit something. Brittany would pay for what she'd done.

"Let me get my computer."

My laptop was five years old but hadn't died on me yet. I brought it back to the couch and told Riley to bring up her Facebook account.

"What are you going to do?" She sniffed.

"Take a picture."

I took two screen shots—a close-up of the post and one that included Brittany Masters' Facebook page banner.

"Riley, do you have this girl's phone number?"

My daughter nodded.

"I want it."

Her eyes rounded. "Are you going to call her?"

"You bet I am."

"*No*, Mom! It'll just make it worse!"

"Worse than this?" I pointed to the computer screen. "She cannot do this to you. This is bullying, and schools don't tolerate it these days. I wouldn't be surprised if Payton Middle had a policy against it."

"You mean she could get in real trouble? Like get suspended or something?"

"Maybe. Let's hope so."

Riley caught her top lip between her teeth and considered the floor. "She'll hate me."

"Right now I don't care what she feels or thinks. I just want her to stop. Don't you?"

Another nod. A small one. I could see the fright in Riley. Was it better to let the lion roar, or roar back and risk its retaliation?

"Call Brittany on your phone now. I'll talk to her."

"I don't know ..."

"Do it."

Riley pulled in her shoulders and hung her head. Reluctantly, then, she tapped the keypad. "Here." She handed the phone to me.

"Hi, Riley, having a nice evening?" Brittany spoke in a taunting singsong. Rage swelled in my chest. And it felt *good*. I wasn't a stained criminal at that moment. I was doing *right*. I was protecting my daughter.

My fingers dug into the couch. "Brittany, this is Mrs. Westling, Riley's mother."

Silence.

"Get your mother on the phone."

"She's not here."

"I think she is."

"No, she's not. She's on a date."

A *date?* Leaving her daughter home by herself?

"Then I will talk to her tomorrow. *After* talking to the principal at your school. In the meantime, I want you to take that picture off your Facebook page right now. And then I want you to post an apology to Riley. You hear me?"

The line went dead. I pulled the cell away from my ear and stared at it. How could a thirteen-year-old be that brazen to an adult?

"She hang up on you?"

I laid the phone down. Closed my eyes and rubbed my neck. My veins churned.

"What do we do now?" Riley asked.

I took a deep breath. "I will go to your school tomorrow and talk to the principal. Show her these pictures. Demand they do something. I'll track down Brittany's mother, too."

Riley lowered her head. "I'm telling you everyone will just hate me more. She's really popular."

I cupped Riley's chin, nudging her head up. The expression on her face made my lungs crack. "You're so pretty. A beautiful girl. One day you'll know that. You *should* know that. Really feel it inside."

Did she see my hypocrisy? I was forty—and had never felt that about myself.

Riley pulled away. "I'm not going to school tomorrow. You can't make me."

How *could* I make her? It wasn't fair. But I needed to meet with the principal. It would be better to have Riley along. To show the school authorities how badly this had upset her.

"I'll just stay home while you're at work."

"I can't leave you alone here all day by yourself."

Riley's mouth trembled. "I'm *not* going, Mom."

"Tell you what." I drew her close. "You will go with me. We'll wait until first hour has already started, so students won't be in the hall. I need you with me in the principal's office. You liked Mrs. Fowler when you met her last week. I did, too. She'll be fair about this. And she'll want to hear your whole story, not just about this picture, but what's been going on every day."

Riley looked away, heaving a sigh. She sniffed. "Even if Brittany stops, I can't make people like me."

I thought of my ex-husband. My father. J.L. "This isn't about making people like you. It's about standing up for yourself. Not letting someone walk all over you."

Riley turned her head and stared me in the eye. I could feel her judgment. Children aren't so easily fooled.

I touched her cheek. "We'll get stronger together. Okay?"

She tore her gaze away, staring at her hands. "Yeah." Her voice sounded small.

My heart surged. I loved her so much. She would have a better life than I had. She *would*.

We lurched through the rest of that evening. I made dinner— after taking Riley's cell phone from her, and the computer. If any other hateful message showed up on Facebook or in a text, *I* would see it, not Riley. Nothing else did show, and within an hour the Facebook post was deleted. But no apology to Riley appeared.

As I moved around the kitchen, I barely felt my own body. My mind churned scenes from the past few hours. I was a *criminal*. An accessory to murder. Every Sheriff's deputy I saw from now on would send ice through my veins. Every day I'd wonder when they would come for me. Then who would care for Riley? Teach her to be strong?

Somehow I had to save myself and her, too.

We ate Riley's chocolate chip cookies for dessert. "You baked them perfectly," I told her.

She pressed her lips together. "I'm going to be a baker when I grow up. I've decided."

"A baker, huh. Sounds good to me. Sounds … *sweet*."

We exchanged a wan smile.

That night I lay in bed staring at the ceiling, sleep long fled. What would J.L. do when I called tomorrow to say I'd be late because of Riley? Would he believe me? What if he thought I'd decided to go to the Sheriff's Office? Would he threaten me? Threaten *Riley*?

Imagine my daughter's life if I did tell law enforcement. She'd be in child custody, her mother in jail for throwing a body off a cliff. Just think of the taunts aimed at Riley then.

Regret flooded me. Why had I done it? Why hadn't I found a way to stand up to J.L.? Tell him *no*?

What tiny piece of evidence would sink me? A missed fingerprint? A hair? An eyewitness?

My life was ruined. And I'd take my daughter down with me.

After midnight the tears came, cold, and raging, and vengeful. When they finally stopped, I was left with a flailing, hopeless determination. There was only one thing I could do. Somehow, some way, I would learn to live with the sin I'd committed. And I'd do anything to cover up the truth. My horrible, unthinkable act must never be found out. For Riley's sake.

And anyone who hurt my daughter would pay.

WEDNESDAY, NOVEMBER 15

CHAPTER 8

The next morning, I dressed for work by rote, my mind thick from lack of sleep. Fear ran deep inside me, an icy stream.

I stood before the mirror, putting on makeup, thoughts tumbling. How long before someone discovered Paula Tellinger was missing? If she lived alone it could be some time. But her car would be found soon. J.L. had made little attempt to hide it.

At 8:00—the time I was supposed to arrive at work—I closed the door to my bedroom to call J.L. at the office. Riley was huddled in her own room, dreading the meeting at school. She'd been too nervous to eat breakfast. My fingers shook as I tapped in the number.

"J.L. Financial." His voice sounded so … normal.

"Hi, it's Cara."

"You okay?"

Just great.

I launched into an explanation about Riley's situation, my words tripping over themselves. I had to convince J.L. I wasn't making up an excuse not to come into work. "I'll get there as soon as I can. But I have to deal with this first."

"I understand." Concern tinged his voice. "This must be awful for Riley. Too bad my daughter's not there to help out."

He'd told me Morgan was in eighth grade at a private school in Hayden.

"What girl did this to Riley?" J.L. asked.

"Brittany Masters. You know that family?"

J.L. made a sound in his throat. "Sheila Masters' kid. Yeah, I know 'em. Sheila wouldn't exactly win Mom of the Year. Divorced a couple of times. Runs around with men a lot. And drinks."

A sliver of sympathy pricked me, but I yanked it out and tossed it aside. Brittany did not deserve my sympathy.

"Listen, Cara, if Riley doesn't want to go to school today, bring her to work. She can read or something. Might be bored, but at least she won't be home by herself all day."

My breath snagged at the very thought. Introduce my daughter to this man, insert him into *her* life? No way.

"Thank you." I kept my tone even. "I'll see you soon."

I clicked off the call and sank onto my bed, gathering my scattered nerves.

Was J.L. truly concerned about my daughter? Who *was* this man? Someone who could kill a woman barehanded, force me to deal with the body—then *apologize*? And later offer to be my friend, my helper?

I dragged myself off the bed, stopping to make one more call—to alert Principal Mary Fowler that Riley and I needed to see her. She agreed to meet with us as soon as we arrived.

Payton Middle School was only two blocks from our rental, an easy walk home for Riley in the afternoons. She and I did not speak on the short drive. When we pulled into the school parking lot she seemed to shrink into herself.

"Come on." I brushed hair off her face. "Let's do this. It'll help, you'll see."

My laptop lay on the back seat. I carried it into the school building. Riley trailed behind, her head down.

The principal was quick to usher us into her office. We'd been there a little over a week earlier, filling out paperwork on Riley's first day of school. Mary Fowler was a petite woman in perhaps her fifties, with French manicured nails and thick brown hair to her shoulders. She had a caring, approachable manner about her, clearly loving her job and the students.

I perched on a chair in front of her desk, Riley seated next to me. Spewing indignation, I told the principal what had happened. Showed her the screen shots on my computer.

Mary Fowler's face pinched. "Oh, Riley, I am so sorry. I just can't imagine …" She shook her head. "This is not a typical Payton welcome; I can tell you that."

"There's more." I looked to Riley. "Tell her what's been going on at school every day for the past week."

Riley's voice was low at first, her words hard formed. I wanted to cry, watching her. I knew that sense of shame all too well, the self-assumed guilt from being traumatized. But after a few minutes Mary Fowler's empathetic listening gave Riley courage. She related all the names Brittany and others had called her, showing the principal their cruel texts. I leaned toward her, nodding, pouring silent encouragement into her. *That's it, Riley. Stand up for yourself. Be strong.*

When my daughter finished, she slumped against the back of her chair, spent.

I turned to the principal. "What are you going to do about this?"

She raised her eyebrows. "We have a zero tolerance policy here against bullying. And cyber bullying is certainly a part of that. Brittany will be suspended, that I can tell you for certain. I'll meet with the other girls before determining what to do about them. I'll also have a meeting with all of their parents." Mrs. Fowler studied Riley. "I'd like to have a meeting with you and the girls also. So they can apologize to you."

Riley looked at the floor, her face paling. I patted her arm.

"Would you like me to arrange that, Riley?"

My daughter shook her head.

"You sure?" Mary Fowler's tone was kind. "Why not?"

Riley shrugged.

"Come on, talk to me."

Riley's fear seeped into my skin, and I *knew*. I understood the feeling of doom and hopelessness. Could taste it.

Depression descended over me.

I wanted to fix this. Mary Fowler wanted to fix it. But we couldn't, any more than police could have changed my ex-husband. What would a forced apology do? And what would happen when Brittany returned from her suspension? Even while she was gone, what would her friends whisper to Riley in the corners of the hallway? As they brushed past her on the way to class?

"They'll hate me, Mom."

What had I done here, forcing my daughter to tell on her classmates? Pushing her to "be strong." What had I really accomplished? Brittany would be punished—so much for my sense of revenge. But my daughter would still be an outcast. Perhaps more than ever. She'd brought trouble on a popular girl. It would all be *her* fault.

My heart turned over. Why had I ever believed we could rise above the things life kept throwing at us?

"I just don't want to." Riley's words were barely audible.

Mary Fowler sighed. "All right, I won't push it."

I rose, wanting *out* of there. "I appreciate your listening. And your responses. I'm going to take Riley home for today. I don't think she's ready to face these girls yet."

The principal stood to shake my hand. "Thanks for coming in. We'll be in touch. And, Riley, I do hope you'll be happy here."

Riley gave a tiny nod and pushed off her chair. "Thank you."

Back in the car, she and I took a minute to breathe.

"Thanks for not making me stay." She wiped a tear on her cheek.

"Yeah." I touched her hair. "I'm not happy about you staying home alone, though. We'll check in with each other throughout the day, okay?"

"Well, keep your phone near you." Accusation tinged Riley's tone. "Not like yesterday."

Her words sent scenarios clacking through my head like falling Dominoes—the Sheriff's Office looking at my phone, seeing the unanswered calls, asking where I'd been at the crucial hour Paula disappeared ....

That one detail could drag Riley into this—into what I'd done. What if they demanded to question her?

Dread pitted my lungs.

"Mom?"

I managed a crooked smile. "I'm fine." I started the car. "Let's get you home."

It was so hard to leave Riley at the house. All alone, with little to do but watch daytime TV. "Call me whenever you need, okay?" I cupped her face in my palms. "I'll be right by the phone."

"Okay."

Blinking back tears, I left for work.

Five minutes later, trembling inside, I walked into J.L.'s offices—and saw him standing near my desk, talking to a man in a sheriff's deputy uniform.

My legs went numb.

"Cara, good morning." J.L. spoke before the man could open his mouth. "Meet Eric Chandler, been with the Kootenai County Sheriff's Office for years." J.L. clapped the deputy on the shoulder. "Eric wanted to talk to us about Paula Tellinger—remember the woman who came in yesterday? Apparently, she's missing."

CHAPTER 9

Deputy Chandler greeted me with a nod. "Good to meet you." He looked to be in his mid-forties, maybe six feet tall and solidly built, with a square face and blue eyes. Dark hair. A nice looking man.

No monster could have scared me more.

"Hello."

Could he see my face pale, the beat of my heart under my coat? I walked to the desk and put down my purse. Leaned against the solid wood for support.

"So what's happened, Eric?" J.L. folded his arms, looking so calm and collected.

The deputy's words spilled over me, lacquering my skin with sweat. Paula Tellinger's car had been discovered early this morning near the side of a dirt road off Highway 95. It was unlocked. Her keys and purse were gone. Same with her cell phone. Nothing about the vehicle looked unusual—other than its being abandoned on a rural road. No one had heard from Paula. She hadn't come home last night, according to her roommate, Linda Gladstone. Which hadn't worried Linda much—until someone from the Sheriff's Office told her about Paula's car. Linda reported the last time she'd seen her roommate was yesterday afternoon. Paula told her she was headed downtown to "have it out with J.L." She was clearly mad about something. She said she'd be home afterward.

Eric Chandler shrugged. "Normally we'd give this kind of thing a little more time. Maybe she's just with a friend. But her car being left out there … It looked suspicious enough that I figured I'd come talk to you."

J.L. shook his head. "Strange, isn't it. Even for Paula. So—no sign of a struggle or something in the vehicle?"

"Not on the surface. We're towing it to the forensic lot to look over."

My throat closed. I pictured myself in Paula's Hyundai, my gloved hands wiping away fingerprints with her scarf. For the hundredth time I asked myself—where was the one I'd missed? Had I left a hair behind? Or any kind of DNA?

My cheeks felt hot. How could I possibly act normal? Surely the deputy saw my guilt.

But—Riley. My daughter, home alone, who so needed her mom to return.

My back straightened.

"Did she come here, J.L.?" Chandler pulled out a notebook and pen.

"Yeah, she was here, all right."

"She a client of yours?"

"No."

"Why was she here?"

"Her ex-boyfriend's a client. Vince Rayle. You talk to him?"

"We've tried. Apparently he's out of town."

J.L. pushed up his lower lip. "Hm." As if he questioned that fact.

I shot him a look.

"Why was Paula here?" Deputy Chandler wrote in his notebook.

J.L. spread his hands. "That's a good question. She stomped in here like she owned the place, hopping mad. I took her in my office and closed the door. She accused me of losing a lot of Vince's money. Called me a bunch of names I won't repeat. Why she thought she should accost me like that, I don't know. First, it's not her money, it's Vince's. Second, I've done just fine by him in preparing his taxes and as an investor—he'll tell you that, so I don't even know what she's talking about. Third, his financial affairs are none of her business. They were together for seven years. Best I can figure, she's doing everything she can to get him back. And somehow she figured coming after me would impress him." J.L. shook his head. "Woman's always been a little off."

Deputy Chandler's head was down as he wrote. I exchanged a quick glance with J.L. How much of his story was true? *"Paula threatened me,"* he'd told me last night. *"Threatened my family."* Why would she do that?

The deputy looked up. "Have you talked to Vince since she was here?"

"No. I didn't see the need. She's not gonna get any proprietary information about his accounts out of me, and as far as I know, he just wants to be done with her. He's bound to be embarrassed that she was even here."

Eric Chandler scratched his chin. "Okay. Back to Paula, what time did she leave?"

J.L. considered the ceiling. "I don't know, maybe some time after 4:00." He focused on me. "You know?"

I pretended to think about it. "It was about 4:30. I remember looking at the clock."

Deputy Chandler made a note. "She say where she was going?"

"No." I started to unbutton my coat, needing some busy work. My fingers felt clumsy.

"What was she wearing?"

My hands slowed. I forced them to keep moving. A warning bell clanged in my head. What should I say—red sweater or blue? Whatever answer came out of my mouth would go in the record. I couldn't take it back. What if that became the one detail that tripped us up? I fought the instinct to look to J.L. for help.

"Jeans and boots," I said. "A sweater—I don't remember the color. And a white scarf—I do remember that."

"A scarf?" The deputy was writing.

"Yes." The words came more freely now, my lips cranking out the lies. "When she left she had it over her head and the sides crossed at the front of her neck, with the ends hanging down her back." I illustrated with my hands.

Eric Chandler nodded. He looked at me, his gaze holding mine for a second too long. It bore right through me. "Anything else you can think of?"

"No." I managed a little smile. "I'm sorry. I hope you find her."

"I do, too. By the way, I need your phone number and address."

I blinked.

"Just routine. I need to be able to follow up with you if necessary."

"Oh. Sure." I gave him the address and my cell number. "I don't have a land line at home."

"Okay." The deputy slipped his notebook and pen into his pocket. "Thank you." He extended his arm to J.L. They shook hands. "Thanks, my man."

"No worries, Eric. And how's that son of yours?" J.L. turned to me. "Trenton's a freshman in college. Can't believe it. Went off to Washington University. I gave that boy his first job when he was ten years old. Had him washing windows at my house." Deputy Chandler smiled. "You sure did. He's great, thanks."

"I didn't see him around much this summer."

"He spent a lot of time in Coeur d'Alene." Deputy Chandler gestured with his chin. "Got himself a girlfriend down there, and you know how that goes."

"A girlfriend, huh." J.L. slapped the deputy on the back. "That oughtta keep him out of trouble. Or get him *in* it."

Both men laughed.

Eric Chandler nodded at me, his eyes warm. "Well, I'll let you two get back to work. Nice to meet you, Cara."

I gave him another smile. "You too."

"Thanks for stopping in," J.L. said. "Let me know if you find out anything about Paula."

"I'll do that."

J.L. ushered the man out and closed the door. He took a deep breath and turned to face me.

I froze, feeling like a deer in sudden headlights. Had I said something wrong? Looked too guilty? Should I have said a red sweater? Blue?

Not even twenty-four hours had passed, and already I could not handle this twisted new life. Even worse, I found myself looking to J.L.—the man who'd pulled me into the chaos—for reassurance. Had I done well—*lied* well enough—to please him?

I could barely get out a whisper. "Tell me I didn't just send us both to prison."

CHAPTER 10

Riley slumped on the couch, watching TV with half-glazed eyes. A stupid talk show was on. Her mom said they couldn't afford cable movie channels.

Her phone pinged. A text.

Riley leaned over to look at the cell's lighted screen.

> U A TATTLE TALE NOW MISS PIGGY?
> HOPE NOT OR U BETTER WATCH UR
> BACK.

It was from Stephanie, Brittany's BFF.

Ants crawled up Riley's spine.

Two more texts came.

> SOMEBODY SAW U AND UR MOM GOING
> INTO THE PRINCIPALS OFFICE. LIKE
> WE WOULDN'T HEAR ABOUT THAT?

WHERE ARE U RIGHT NOW? OH I
KNOW. RAN LIKE A CHICKEN TO UR
CAR AND WENT HOME. WE'LL CATCH
UP WITH U LATER. ULL B SORRY.

Riley stared at the phone until it went dark. Her throat got all tight. Now she was in *real* trouble. Now they were going to hurt her.

No way could she go to school tomorrow. Mrs. Fowler couldn't watch over her every minute. Adults just didn't get it. All kinds of things happened when they weren't looking.

Riley hovered over the phone. Should she erase the texts? She didn't want to see them anymore. But Mom would want her to keep them as evidence—so she could tattle again.

Look where that had gotten her.

Still, she should keep them. Because once Stephanie found out Brittany was suspended, and she might get in trouble, too, she'd erase them from her own phone. She'd deny she ever sent them.

Riley's cell went off again, this time playing her favorite Miley Cyrus song. A call. Riley went still, her eyes glued to the name on the screen.

Stephanie.

Riley pressed knuckles against her chin, staring at the phone. Just before the song stopped playing, her finger shot out and swiped to answer. She put the cell to her ear. "H-hello."

"Mrs. Fowler just came and took Brittany out of class," Stephanie snapped. "What did you tell her?"

"Nothing."

"You did too, you liar! Brittany didn't do anything to you, none of us did. You can't prove *anything*. And we will never be your friends, got that? *Never!*"

The phone went dead.

Riley threw it on the couch. Two thoughts tangled in her head. One—she was done in this town. She knew it. This wouldn't get better, no matter what her mom or some principal did. So she might as well live with that reality. Two—was Stephanie stupid? *"You can't prove anything."* Good thing Riley hadn't just erased those texts—or any of the past ones she'd gotten. Good thing her mom had taken a screen shot of that Facebook post. Brittany and her dumb friends could get rid of everything they wanted. Wouldn't change the proof Riley had.

Like people could just get rid of evidence on their end and think everything was good.

And so what if she couldn't make these girls like her? She didn't want them as friends now anyway. They were *pathetic*.

Riley and her mom had to move out of this town. Now.

She snatched up her phone to call her mother.

CHAPTER 11

I stood before J.L., heart hammering. Before he could respond, my cell phone went off in my purse.

Riley.

I wavered, looking from J.L. to my desk.

"Is that your daughter? Answer it."

"But did I do okay?"

"Yes. Answer the phone."

Yes. He said yes! Still, my hands couldn't stop trembling as I slipped the cell from my bag. "Riley, you all right?"

Her words gushed out—new texts, threats that she should "watch her back," and that those girls would *never, ever* be her friends. As for Riley, she didn't care, because she *never, ever* wanted to so much as *see* them again. And she wouldn't, because she *wasn't* going back to school, and we were moving from Payton.

Oh, Riley.

Her pain flowed into me, and I wanted to cry. Just put down the phone and wail, for her and for myself. Less than thirty minutes had passed since I left home. I'd faced an investigating Sheriff's deputy. Lied to him, which had to be another crime. Now this.

J.L. wandered closer, concern on his face. I knew he could hear every word my daughter said.

"Riley—"

"Mom, you have to *listen* to me. This *isn't* going to work. I can't go back there!"

My eyes closed, deep weariness washing over me. What should I *do*?

"Riley, I hear you. I'm so sorry. I'll fix this somehow. We'll go back to Mrs. Fowler—"

"That's not gonna help! And I might not *be* here when you get home!"

Fear shot through me. "What do you mean by that?"

"I'm not staying here, Mom. I'll go live with Dad."

The father who didn't want her. Who'd abandoned us both.

"Riley, I know you're upset right now, but if you'd just calm—"

"Let me talk to her." J.L. thrust out his hand for the phone.

What? I gaped at him.

Riley fell silent. She must have heard him speak.

"Come on, Cara, it'll be all right." J.L. waggled his fingers.

"No."

"*Cara.*"

I couldn't let Riley hear him bully me. Reluctantly, I put the phone in his palm.

He gave me a little nod.

"Hello, Riley? This is J.L. Larrett, your mom's boss." His voice sounded reassuring. Fatherly. "I want you to call me J.L." He held the top part of the phone away from his ear far enough to allow me to hear Riley.

A pause. "Hi."

"I hear you're having some trouble at school. Didn't Mrs. Fowler help you? I know her. I know everybody in town. She's a nice woman."

"Yeah, but ... she can't really help." Riley sounded embarrassed. I could imagine her reaction when I got home—*Like I want to talk about this with your boss?*"

"I get it." J.L. wandered over to an armchair and sat down. I hovered near my desk. What was this? I did *not* want him talking to my child.

"You know I have a daughter your age?" J.L. leaned back in the chair, legs spread. So casual, as if this was any regular day, a normal conversation. "Her name's Morgan. She goes to a private school in Hayden. Real sweet girl. I'm sure she'd love to meet you."

No! I shook my head hard.

J.L. ignored me.

I couldn't hear Riley's response. J.L. had moved too far away.

"Well, I can make sure you two get together. But this school situation bothers me. We can't let that go on. Your mom's doing real well here at work, and I don't want to lose her. I want both of you to be happy in Payton."

Happy? The things I'd had to do because of this man. The person I'd become. "J.L., stop, let me talk to her." I strode to him, my hand gesturing. He waved me away.

"What I'm thinking is, Riley, maybe Payton Middle just isn't the right school for you."

"Don't tell her that!" I hissed.

"Sometimes if the fit isn't right, it makes more sense to just change clothes, know what I mean? Maybe you ought to try Morgan's school, Hayden Prep."

I shook my head again, sick inside. I couldn't afford a private school.

"Well, don't worry about that, I'll talk to your mom, okay? Main thing is for you to just take it easy today. Let your mom get her work done, and I promise you, we'll figure this out. Meanwhile I suggest you not look at your phone unless your mom calls. Don't take other calls, and *don't* read texts." He blew air through his teeth. "Those dumb girls—you don't need 'em. You're way better than they are."

He was silent for a moment. I looked on, helpless.

"Thatta girl." J.L. smiled. "You hang in there now, and I'll talk to you later."

He clicked off the call and stood. Held out my phone. I snatched it back.

"You shouldn't have said any of that." Tears scratched my eyes. "Why did you even talk to her? She *has* to go back to Payton Middle tomorrow. I hate that, but it's reality. I can't afford a private school."

J.L. waved a hand. "Don't worry about that."

"How can I *not* worry?" Who did this man think he was? My throat tightened. "You had no right to mention an expensive school. Why did you do that? Just to calm her down for now? I'm the one who has to deal with her after work. You have no right to fill her mind with false promises."

J.L. folded his arms. "You think that's what I do? Make false promises?"

"I—" I smacked the phone down on my desk, indignation overcoming my fear. Taking advantage of me was one thing. My daughter was something else. "I don't know, J.L. I don't know *who* you are. Mr. Nice Guy who's loved by everyone in town—and just happens to kill women?"

His face flushed. "Keep your voice down."

"You have *me*, okay? You made me do what you wanted, and now I'm ... tied to you. In this horrible way. But let me tell you something right now. You *do not* get my daughter."

He pulled back his head. "What are you talking about, I'm just trying to help."

"You're *not helping*."

J.L. cocked his head. "Did you hear what she said? Those girls are now threatening her physically. 'Watch your back?' And you're going to force her to return to that school?"

Tears spilled from my eyes. "I don't *want* to do that. I'm scared to death for her. But I don't have a choice."

"Yes, you do." J.L.'s tone softened. He took a step toward me. I raised my palms, and he stopped.

We regarded each other warily.

Fear of him suddenly surged back. What was I *doing*? I was the only one who knew the truth about this man. If he'd killed Paula, he could kill me, too.

My legs felt weak. I shuffled around the desk and sank into my chair.

J.L. sighed. "Look. This situation with Riley has to be fixed. So here's what I'm going to do. I'm going to send her to my daughter's school."

What?

"And I'm gonna pay for it."

Was he insane? "I can't let you do that."

"You want her back with those girls who want to beat her up?"

"No! I ..."

"Then let me do it."

"Why would you want to?"

He spread his hands. "I'm a nice guy."

I pressed back against my chair.

J.L. read my expression and looked almost hurt. "You don't know me, Cara. What happened yesterday was terrible. Unplanned and unimaginable. You think I slept last night? You think I'm not upset and shaking today? Just because I don't show it—that means nothing. I'm sorry it happened. I'm devastated it happened. And that I had to bring you into it. I said I'm sorry for that, and I meant it." J.L. stepped closer to the desk. "But now we're not going to talk about it again, you hear? What's done is done. I'm not going to explain myself to you. I'm not going to tell you anything more about Paula, or what she said against my family—my *daughter*— that frightened me so badly to make this happen. We're at *this* point in time now, you and me. We're stuck together in this knowledge, this thing, and we have to deal with it."

My mouth opened but no words came.

"I told you yesterday I would take care of you, and I meant it. Right now that means helping Riley. Hayden Prep is not that expensive a school for me. I can afford to pay another tuition. And that's what I'm going to do. No one but the principal needs to know. I'll write them a check today for tuition through December. And as long as you stay in this job, I'll keep paying—all the way through high school. So you can quit worrying about your daughter and focus on your work here. And I promise you Morgan will be a good friend to Riley. She's a sweet girl. Not a mean bone in her body."

I shook my head.

J.L. spread his hands. "For the sake of your daughter, how can you say no?"

I stared at him, emotions colliding in my head. If everything he said was true, it would be an incredible gift to Riley. A new start, new friends. That would raise her from depression, make her *believe* in herself. But it would also mean even more dependency on J.L. His daughter—my daughter's friend. Riley's schooling—funded by him. It meant not leaving this job. It meant accepting a huge gift *because* of what I'd done for him.

A bribe?

J.L. watched the internal battle play out on my face. "Cara." His voice softened. "What is there to think about here?"

Did he really not get it? Or was he just a master manipulator?

"But Payton Middle is just a few blocks from where we live. How would Riley get home?"

"Rachelle will bring her home. My wife. She picks up Morgan every day anyway. She can take Riley in the mornings, too, if you want."

Another tie to him—his wife driving Riley to and from school. Would there be anything in my life J.L. Larrett wasn't involved in?

"What if Morgan doesn't like Riley? You can't make girls that age be friends."

"She will. Trust me."

How could he be so sure? Did Morgan do everything her dad said—out of fear? Or was she really that goodhearted?

Would she be a *real* friend to Riley? How could I take the chance of a brand new set of girls turning on her?

"They'll be friends, Cara. Morgan will introduce Riley to everyone. It's a small school environment. Very warm and caring. She'll fit right in."

"She'd still have to deal with Brittany and her gang around town. Payton's only, what—fifteen thousand people? It's not like they won't run into each other."

J.L. pierced me with a look. "We can't fix everything at once, Cara. One thing at a time."

I felt like Paula Tellinger, teetering on the edge of a cliff. About to fall so far I could never climb out.

Did I have no self-worth left?

But ... Riley. Crying alone at home, scared to death to return to school. How could I deny her the chance to be happy?

Even as my mouth opened, I did not know what I would say. "Okay."

"You'll let me do it?"

I nodded.

J.L.'s mouth spread in a big smile. "Well, now, I'm glad to hear that. And I'm happy for her. For you, too."

Something inside me folded in half. I smiled back, swallowing against the tightness in my throat. "Thank you. Riley will be so excited."

My boss blew out a satisfied breath. "Why don't you call now and tell her? I'll let you off early this afternoon so you can take her to school and get her enrolled. Meanwhile I'll phone the principal, let her know you're coming.

"You're sure she can get in?"

"They won't say no to me." J.L. headed for his office. "Let's get this set up, then we need to get to work. Tell Riley you'll be home at 3:30."

J.L. strode into his office and closed the door. I stared after him, numb, relieved, and weak with fear. Now I'd done it. Plummeted over the cliff.

What would I find at the bottom?

Eric Chandler
Paula Tellinger—Questions
11:00 a.m., 11/15

P's car—dirt splashed on doors, tires. Where from?

Car pointed toward Highway 95. Where coming from?

Why did P. confront J.L.?

Cara—J.L.'s new assistant—nervous. Past run-in with law? CHECK.

Vince Rayle out of town? CHECK.

Security cameras starting at 4:30 p.m.—P. driving car from J.L.'s office. CHECK.

CHAPTER 12

"You mean it, Mom? *Really?*" Crazy excitement wanted to pick Riley right off the couch and dance her around. She couldn't let it. Because it was probably too good to be true ...

"Yes, really. It's the best thing for you, I think. J.L.—Mr. Larrett—is letting me off early. I'll pick you up at 3:30 to take you over to the school for registration, so be ready."

Something in her mom's tone. Worry? Riley leaned forward, frowning. "But you said we don't have any money. How can you afford to send me to a private school?"

"I ... we didn't."

"So—what? Now we do?"

Her mom hesitated. "No."

"Then ..."

"Don't worry about it, Riley. All you need to think about is—you get to go."

"I know but ..." Mr. Larrett had told Riley about the school, like this was all his idea. And that thing he'd said—*I promise you, we'll figure this out.*

"Is Mr. Larrett paying for it?"

"Riley, I don't ... We don't need to talk about this."

"But I want to *know*! I don't want to start a new school and have everything be great, and then hear we can't afford it anymore!"

"That won't happen."

"How do you know?"

Her mom sighed. "Because it's being paid for."

Riley sat back. It had to be J.L. But why? Some man she didn't even know was doing this for *her*?

"So your boss paid for it?"

Another pause. "Yes."

This was *amazing*. "Why don't you sound happier?"

"I *am* happy."

Didn't sound much like it. Mom should have that lightness in her voice, like when she told Riley she'd found a job in Idaho.

"Listen, Riley, I'm just surprised, is all. And I just ... I want this to work for you. I so want *you* to be happy."

Riley couldn't remember what that felt like. "This was all Mr. Larrett's idea, wasn't it."

"Yes."

"Mom, you have a really cool boss!"

Her mom made some sound, like she was trying to laugh.

"And his daughter. Morgan. She's in my grade, right?"

"I think so. From what I hear, it's a small school, so you'll probably meet everyone pretty quickly."

Morgan would be her friend. That's what her dad had said, anyway. "Do you believe him that she's nice? That she'll like me?"

Because what if she didn't? What if the same thing happened all over again?

"He says she will, Riley. He promised me she's a sweet girl. Like you. Think how you'd treat someone new to your school, who didn't know anyone."

Riley swallowed hard. She so wanted to believe it. Well, she did believe it. She had to. Because going back to Payton Middle was not an option.

The excitement swirled again inside her. Riley couldn't hold it back any longer. She jumped up, all the fear and worry and hate she'd felt over Brittany and the other girls melting away. She wouldn't have to deal with them anymore. Wouldn't have to look at their stuck-up faces.

"I'll be ready at 3:30. I can't *wait!*"

Riley tapped off the call and threw her cell on the couch. She danced out from behind the coffee table, threw her hands in the air and twirled around. "Yes, yes, *yes!*" Ha-ha on Brittany and Stephanie and the rest of them. *They'd* be the ones in trouble, suspended from school. Well, at least Brittany. Maybe Stephanie, too. Maybe they'd get in even more trouble when Mrs. Fowler found out they'd driven Riley away for good.

She glanced at the old round clock on the wall. Ten-thirty. Five hours left. That would take forever.

What should she wear? She ran into her room and started pulling out different jeans and tops. Nothing was new. If only she had the money and time to go shopping. The first day of school at Payton Middle she'd worn the newest jeans she had and a pale blue long sleeved top with lace at the neck. She'd looked pretty in that. Hadn't she?

Riley tore off her clothes and put on the jeans and shirt. Then stood in front of the long mirror on her wall, turning side to side. She looked good in the jeans, not all that fat.

She went back to her closet. Or what if she wore—

Her cell phone pinged in the living room. A text.

Riley stilled.

Brittany? Stephanie?

Well, so what, they couldn't hurt her anymore. In fact, time to block them from her phone. Forever. No calls. And no more stupid "friends" on Facebook and Snapchat.

Riley stalked to the living room to yank up her phone.

The screen had darkened. She swiped across it—and saw a text from a number she didn't recognize.

HI RILEY. THIS IS MORGAN. MY
DAD SAID UR COMING TO MY SCHOOL
TODAY TO REGISTER. GREAT! MEET U
AT THE PRINCIPALS OFFICE.

Riley's mouth opened. Morgan was already being nice. Before she could reply, another text came.

FRIEND ME ON FB. AND LOOK UP THE
PAGE FOR HAYDEN PREPARATORY. SEE
U SOON!

Riley sucked in a breath. She flopped down on the couch and hunched over her phone, tapping the Facebook app. She looked up Morgan's page. Wow. Morgan was pretty. Long black hair with straight bangs. Big brown eyes with long lashes. She looked like a model. Riley so wanted to hang around with someone who was pretty *and* nice.

She sent a Facebook friend request, hoping Morgan would see it soon. Riley couldn't wait to read her posts. Next she looked up the school's page. The banner showed a building of wood and stone. Looked good. Riley clicked the *like* button.

She lost track of time as she scrolled down the school's page, reading posts and seeing the faces of different students. A lot of cute boys went there. And everyone looked happy. The teachers looked fun. It all looked *great*.

Riley couldn't wait to start there tomorrow.

When she finally lifted her head, it was past noon. Her stomach growled. First time she'd felt like eating all day.

Before she went into the kitchen, she had one more thing to do on her phone. With a satisfied smirk, she blocked the numbers for Brittany, Stephanie, and their gang of friends.

There. She threw down her phone and stood. "Forget *all* of you. I have a *new* life now."

Humming, she headed for the kitchen to make some lunch.

CHAPTER 13

Within five minutes J.L. was back near my desk, telling me about Hayden Prep. He'd talked to the principal, Ellen Grunelle. She was expecting me and Riley at 4:00.

J.L. looked pleased with himself, a benefactor changing a young girl's life. He stood with feet apart, one hand on his hip and the other gesturing as he extolled the virtues of Hayden Prep. The low number of students per class, the excellence of its teachers. I tried to focus on his words. But I was having trouble thinking. My body still felt heavy from lack of sleep, the gears of my brain running on a drained battery.

Had J.L. done this for Riley to help keep me under his thumb? Or was it penance?

My insides felt ripped in two. Part of me was so relieved and grateful that Riley had been saved. The other part could not believe I'd sold my soul for this new plan. And—what if things fell apart for her *again*?

"… perfect record regarding higher education," J.L.'s bushy eyebrows rose. "One hundred percent of the graduates go to college …"

Purse. Out of nowhere the thought sideswiped me. My mouth opened, then closed. We weren't supposed to talk about Paula anymore.

"… and they do a great job—"

"J.L." The words rushed out. "Did you take care of the purse and phone and scarf?"

His words cut off mid-sentence. He blinked, then narrowed his eyes. "I told you I would."

"Where did you put them?"

"In a dumpster."

"How do you know you weren't seen?"

"I wasn't."

"How do you *know?*"

"I *wasn't.*" He tilted his head and glared at me.

What was I doing? He could take away this gift as quickly as he'd given it. "J.L., I'm sorry. Truly."

"Cara." He planted his palms on my desk and leaned toward me, face grim. "You need to start trusting me."

"I … do."

"I cannot have a partner who *does not trust me.*"

He held my gaze, as if daring me to look away. My stomach fluttered.

"I do. Really. I'm sorry I asked."

J.L. let out a long breath, then straightened.

The office phone on my desk rang. I jumped. J.L. threw it an irritated look.

I hesitated. "Should I answer it?"

He waved a hand. "Go ahead. Just—I'm not here."

I took a steadying breath and picked up the receiver. "Good morning, J.L. Financial."

"Is the old man in?" The male voice was rough and steely, like a heavy smoker's.

"I'm sorry, no. May I take a message?"

"Did Paula come by there yesterday?"

I stilled, my gaze shooting to J.L. "I'm sorry, who is this?"

"Vince Rayle."

Paula's ex.

Be calm, Cara.

My hand reached for a pen. "Mr. Rayle, I'll be happy to take a message for you." I looked to J.L. for approval. He nodded.

A huff came over the phone. "I don't *want* to leave a message. I need to know if Paula was there. Her roommate called me, says she's missing. And the last thing Paula told her—she was going over to your office."

J.L. made a face, as if he'd heard the man's words. I shook my head at him—*what am I supposed to say?* J.L. pointed toward his office and mouthed, *"Put him through."*

I nodded. "Oh, wait, J.L.'s just coming in the door." I lowered the phone, knowing Vince Rayle could still hear me. "Morning, J.L. Vince Rayle's on the line."

"Okay."

J.L. closed his office door behind him as his line began to ring. I replaced my receiver in its cradle.

Silence.

I stared at my computer, at a loss. How to understand the different sides of J.L.? Giving boss ... controller of my life. Loving father ... murderer. I *had* to understand him in order to stay one step ahead. I needed to placate him, give him no reason to be mad at me. He'd gotten angry at Paula—and look what happened to her.

The irony. Jeff was finally out of my life—and here I was again, struggling to keep peace with an abusive man to save myself. Some bright new start.

My gaze roamed over the office. I had work to be done. Piles of tax packets sat on the floor, needing to be addressed. There were bills to pay and record. I was supposed to make out the checks, J.L. signing them.

But every deed I performed for this man from now on would be like shoveling dirt into an open grave. Covering over our sin. Even now I could stop. I could walk out the door and find Deputy Eric Chandler. Tell him the truth.

And I would go to jail. Lose my daughter.

I'm not a bad person. I'd just ... fallen into a trap. And I saw no way out.

With a deep sigh I picked up a pile of tax packets and set them on my desk.

CHAPTER 14

At noon I went home for lunch to check up on Riley. She had four or five tops and pants pulled from her closet and lying on her bed. Her cheeks were flushed, and she couldn't stop smiling. "I'm wearing these tomorrow." She pointed to a pink top and a pair of jeans.

I took her face in my hands. "You will look so pretty."

She grinned.

I couldn't remember when I'd seen her so excited. Was it really only hours ago that she'd dragged herself behind me into Payton Middle School?

Without Paula's death, Riley might still be stuck in that school and miserable.

What a dark, indefensible thought. How *could* I? My mind shoved it away.

During the lunch break I called Principal Fowler at Payton Middle to inform her Riley would be changing schools. I left the house shortly before 1:00, telling Riley I'd be back in two and a half hours. She practically skipped me to the door.

Hayden Prep had better be good, I told myself as I made the short drive back to work. If Riley came crashing down again, how would she ever pull out of it?

An hour after I returned to my desk, Deputy Eric Chandler walked through the door. Second time in less than four hours. My body went cold.

J.L. was in his office with the door closed.

"Hello, Mr. Chandler."

As he walked toward me, I heard the faint creak of his gear. Such a small sound. But it screamed to me of who he was.

"Sorry to bother you again." He smiled.

"You're not bothering me." My throat felt pasty. "Have you found that woman? Paula?" I laid my hands in my lap so he wouldn't see them shake.

"No. But I have a few more questions for J.L. Is he in?"

I nodded. Somehow I managed to pick up my phone and hit the intercom button.

"Yes?"

"Eric Chandler is here to see you."

Silence. Tension pulsed over the line. "Be right out."

J.L.'s door opened, his boots scuffing as he crossed the carpet toward my desk. "Eric, my man, twice in one day." He drew up in front of the deputy, his fingers hooking on to his belt loops. "Paula musta turned up."

"Afraid not."

J.L. regarded Eric. "You sound like it's serious."

The deputy shook his head. "I don't know what to think about this. And she still could turn up. But it just doesn't look right, you know?"

I wanted to scream at him. *What did you find?*

"We looked the car over some more once we got it to our lot. Still no sign of anything gone wrong. But somebody wiped it clean of prints."

J.L. frowned. "How do you know?"

"There should be fingerprints all over a car. Especially on door handles and near the ignition. On the steering wheel. But—nothing."

J.L.'s eyebrows rose. "No prints anywhere?"

The deputy shrugged. "A few on the backseat doors."

The backseat.

I stopped breathing.

Scenes from the previous night raced through my mind. I saw myself in the car, driving. Furiously rubbing with the scarf. I hadn't wiped down the backseat. Because I'd never touched those doors. I hadn't been back there at all, I would swear to it.

Right? *Right?*

J.L. pushed air through his teeth. "What did that crazy woman do? She must have staged this. She could have run off with someone and made it look like something happened to her."

"Any guess why she'd do that?"

"Probably to get back at Vince. Make him feel guilty that something happened to her. I wouldn't put that past Paula one bit."

Chandler buffed his forehead. "Yeah. Maybe."

"Don't think so?"

"Could be. I think she's capable of that. I got called out to her and Vince's house a few times myself for domestic issues. Arrested him twice and her once. The woman's got a temper. And she strikes me as kind of ... scheming."

J.L. nodded. "You're right about that."

Had I touched those back doors? My head floated somewhere above my body.

"So those prints in the backseat," J.L. said. "If you arrested her before, you've got her prints. Do they match?"

"No. We don't know whose they are. Doesn't mean much at this point. Could just be someone who rode in her car."

"Yeah." J.L. regarded the deputy.

Eric Chandler focused out the window. "I'm just trying to figure—if she staged this whole thing to leave town, why come to you about Vince's finances right before leaving? I could see her doing one or the other. But both—I'm thinking maybe there's a connection."

A tingling started in my legs, moving up to my back.

"Any thoughts, J.L.? Anything she said to you that you didn't think to tell me this morning?"

J.L. stared at the carpet, frowning. A forever moment passed. I could almost hear the cogs in his head turning—should he lie and make something up?

He blew out a long breath and looked to Eric Chandler. "I can't think of anything. But you're right, her disappearance does make her visit here look even more strange. What *was* her point in coming? Even if I had lost a lot of Vince's money through bad investments, it's not like I'd write him a personal check to cover it. And she didn't seem to expect that. It's like she just wanted to have it on record that she gave me grief about it. I still think she did it to get back in good graces with Vince."

Second time I'd heard that explanation—and it didn't sound any more plausible than before. Did Eric Chandler believe it?

Why had Paula come here?

"Maybe she went to see Vince after leaving here," J.L. said. "You talk to him yet, Eric?"

"Yeah, just a little while ago. Said he's on his way back into town. That he was at his cabin up at Priest River last night."

J.L. raised his chin, as if processing the information.

"He called you, didn't he?" Chandler asked. "He said he'd talked to you."

"Yeah, he did. He just ... didn't mention he was at his cabin." The way J.L. said it—as if Vince Rayle's failure to mention that fact was surprising. Maybe even suspicious.

Eric Chandler rubbed his face. "Well, I told you this morning he said he was out of town."

"Yeah. Sure."

The two men looked at each other. Uneasiness soured the air.

"Anything else you think I can help you with?" J.L. asked.

"Don't think so. Thanks." The deputy turned toward me. "Good to see you again, ma'am."

"You too, Mr. Chandler."

"Call me Eric."

I managed a smile. "Okay. Eric."

He smiled back, then headed for the door. "We'll talk to Vince when he gets here, J.L. Should be soon. Other than that, not too much we can do right now. I still have half a mind Paula will turn up. Like nothing ever happened."

J.L. laughed. "Then *you'll* catch it from her. For taking her car."

Eric Chandler disappeared through the door. Once again I faced J.L., panic firing through my veins.

"Were you in that backseat?" His voice was low.

"No. I never went back there." I felt sweat on my forehead. "I didn't wipe it down because *I never went back there*! I swear!"

"Okay, okay." J.L. held up both hands.

I hugged my arms across my chest. "I don't know how to do this." The words turned thick. "Every time I see a deputy. Every time Paula's name is mentioned ..."

"You're doing just fine." J.L. strode closer to my desk and stared down at me, the stern parent to the child. "Hear me? You're *fine.* You want to talk about the alternative? You want to even *think* what would happen—"

"No!" I shook my head hard. "I just ... You're right. I *am* fine. I just ... got scared."

Terrified of being found out, yes. Even more petrified of what J.L. might do if he thought he couldn't trust me.

"Don't worry." I looked up at him. "I'll be okay. I'll be great."

J.L. held my eyes in a long, assessing gaze. "Just think about your daughter."

"I *am.* Thank you. For school, again, I mean. Thank you so much. I'm good now. I won't let you down."

J.L. lifted his chin and let out a long breath through his nose. "My work's piling up in there. I got a lot of things I need to do for clients."

"Go." I waved a hand.

As J.L. neared his office door, he turned back. "Eric likes you, you know."

I shot him a blank look. "Huh?"

"He does. I can tell. He's not married. His wife left him three years ago. He's ready for a new relationship."

I couldn't think of a thing to say.

"He'd be a great catch, Cara."

What? The deputy investigating the disappearance of the woman J.L. had murdered. The woman whose body I'd helped get rid of. Was J.L. insane?

"I ... I'm not ready ..."

He shrugged. "I know you haven't been divorced that long. But if the right person comes along ..."

What was I supposed to say?

My boss shifted on his feet. "Look. Just think about it. If he happens to ask you out, don't say no."

This, too? On top of everything else J.L. controlled in my life, now he wanted to tell me who to date?

"Cara. I see that look on your face. Listen. You've heard that saying, 'Keep your friends close and your enemies closer.' Not that he suspects you or me. But he's a good deputy. And he's looking into places where we don't want him to look. He's not going to find anything. But if he did, if he got even the tiniest bit suspicious about some piece of this, it would be good to keep him close. So we'd hear about it. Maybe he'd talk to you."

"He's already talking to *you*. You're his friend."

"He won't keep coming around here every day. He and I go days without seeing each other. But if you and he got close ..."

Inside me another iron door slammed. My prison cell was getting smaller. Rattier.

"I'm not that good an actress, J.L."

His mouth spread in a slow smile. "You're better than you think."

That was not a compliment.

J.L. pushed back his shoulders in an exaggerated stretch. "Nothing for you to decide now. Just think about it for when the time comes. I'm sure you'll do the right thing."

He gave me a final nod and turned toward his office.

Eric Chandler
Paula Tellinger Disappearance—Questions
2:30 p.m., 11/15

Car—backseat fingerprints. Whose?

Car otherwise wiped clean. Why?

Blonde hair—driver's seat. Paula's?

Blonde hair—trunk. Paula's?

Chip of white fingernail polish—trunk. Paula's?

Dirt on car doors, tires—from forest service road?

CHAPTER 15

That afternoon a reporter called from the local newspaper, *The Coeur d'Alene Press*. He said his name was Greg Bonhoffer, and he wanted information on Paula Tellinger's meeting with J.L.

Once again my tongue tied as I sought for lies.

How had Bonhoffer heard Paula was here?

My fingers curled around the receiver. J.L. and I should have thought about reporters. Planned what to say. It was one more event to make me realize he and I couldn't cover everything. Somewhere down the line something was going to crack.

"I'm sorry, I'm not able to give out information about client meetings here." Which was true. Meetings were confidential.

"How about Mr. Larrett, is he in?"

Of course the reporter wouldn't be pushed aside that easily.

"Just a moment."

I put the call on hold and buzzed J.L.

He made an impatient sound in his throat. "Tell him I'm not available."

"He'll call back. What do I say then?"

"We're not talking to reporters, Cara."

"I get that, but ... Won't we sound like we're hiding something if we refuse to talk?"

"What exactly would you like me to say?"

"I'm not telling you to say anything! I just want to know how to handle this. Tell *me* what to say."

J.L. sighed. "Tell him we are not speaking to reporters. We have talked with law enforcement and told them everything we know. End of story. Got it?"

Anxiety kicked around in my stomach. First Riley, then Eric, now this. I was not doing well placating J.L.

"Okay."

I returned to Greg Bonhoffer and repeated the words.

"Can you just confirm Ms. Tellinger was there?"

"I'm sorry—no."

He asked a few more leading questions. I dodged, then finally said, "I have to go now." And hung up.

Veins prickling, I sat staring at the antler coat tree. Would that be the end of the reporter's calls? What if he came to the office— would he see the guilt on my face? Weren't journalists trained to be suspicious?

Law enforcement people certainly were. Had Eric Chandler sensed something about me? Had he come back here just to see my reaction?

My nerves had barely settled when I faced a second confrontation.

A man entered the office. He was short, maybe five-eight, and muscled. Thick dark hair. Entitlement emanated from him, as if he stood on familiar territory. He strode past my desk without a word, heading toward J.L.'s office.

"I'm sorry—do you have an appointment?"

He swung toward me, scowling. "I don't need an appointment."

I recognized the voice. Vince Rayle.

He and Paula Tellinger—and their attitudes. They deserved each other.

"Mr. Rayle, let me—"

Vince barreled on, shoving J.L.'s door open. "I just came from talking to that Sheriff's deputy, Eric Chandler. Thinks he's hot stuff, asking me all kinda questions. Like *I* know where Paula is."

"Well, hello, Vince," J.L.'s voice filtered around the corner. "Nice to see you, too."

"*Why* are they on me like this? They're really ticking me off."

J.L.'s chair creaked. "Come on in and sit down. No need to get yourself all worked up."

My boss appeared on the threshold. He shot me a look before closing the door.

CHAPTER 16

The Hayden Prep building looked even nicer than in the Facebook picture. Riley's head swiveled back and forth, taking in the wide door entrance and all the windows as her mom parked the car. Riley pictured kids inside those windows, in the classrooms. That would be *her* tomorrow. Sitting there, like she belonged.

She *would* belong here. She could feel it. Morgan already sounded like a friend.

Riley had texted her when they left home. Morgan said she'd stay after school to meet them when they got there.

"You ready?" Mom smiled.

"Yeah." Riley looked down at herself. At the last minute she'd changed from the pink top, going back to the blue one. She could see the lacey cuffs peeking out of her coat sleeve.

As Riley and her mom walked up the sidewalk, the school's door opened and Morgan jumped out. She was hugging herself tightly against the cold—no coat on. "I couldn't wait until you got inside!" She grinned.

Her smile made the day feel like summer.

Morgan hugged Riley. "So glad you're here."

Riley nodded, her throat lumpy. "Me too."

Like the school building, Morgan was even better in person. Her long black hair was shiny, and her large brown eyes looked like warm chocolate. Light energy floated from her. Sort of like bubbles.

Riley's mom and Morgan greeted each other. "Thank you for helping us," Mom told her. "And for waiting. That was really sweet of you."

"Oh, no problem. It's fun to help, since you work with my dad." Morgan said that last word with pride in her voice.

Riley didn't exactly feel pride when she thought about her own father. Plus, Riley wouldn't even be here if Morgan's dad hadn't paid her tuition.

J.L. Larrett had to be the best man in the world.

Did Morgan know he'd paid Riley's way? Please no. She didn't want anybody to think she was a charity case.

Morgan led them through an empty hall toward the principal's office. "It's quiet right now because everyone's gone home." She tucked her hand beneath Riley's arm as she chattered on. "I'll introduce you around tomorrow. You'll like everyone here. It's the best school, way better than Payton Middle." She made a face.

Riley glanced back at her mom, who gave her a little smile as if to say—*she talks a lot, huh.* Riley hunched her shoulders—*yeah.*

The principal, Mrs. Grunelle, was really nice. She had a kind face and thick blonde hair. She was tall, and to be truthful—pretty fat. Which wasn't a bad thing, because she made Riley feel skinny. Morgan waited on a small couch outside Mrs. Grunelle's office while Riley's mom signed a bunch of papers. She had brought records from Riley's previous school in Seattle, which she gave to the principal.

Riley had to sign a document, too, promising to obey the school rules. No drugs or cigarettes or alcohol inside or outside of school. No bullying. (Hah!) Respect for all. Grades kept to C or above.

She picked up a pen and signed in her best handwriting.

Mrs. Grunelle handed Riley a list of her scheduled classes. "The eighth grade has fourteen students in all, counting you. That's just below our maximum of fifteen students per teacher, so you all stay together from one class to the next."

Riley looked over the list. Pretty basic. Math, science, history, English, P.E., and geography. Nothing surprising. All the same, a fresh wave of excitement surged through her. School could be fun when you went through the day with friends.

When they came out of Mrs. Grunelle's office, Morgan stood. "My mom's gonna be here in a minute to pick me up. Can you stay and meet her?"

"Yes, I'd like that." Riley's mom smiled.

What a crazy day. Started out so terrible and ended up so good. Morgan's mom soon showed up, and she and Riley's mom walked out into the hall to talk. Morgan's mom was *gorgeous*. She had her daughter's dark hair, and a great figure. She wore jeans and a jacket and boots, looking really cool.

As Morgan rattled on about everybody in eighth grade, Riley only half listened. A weird feeling started coming over her, like all of this was too good to be true. What were the two moms talking about? How Riley had been bullied? She didn't want Morgan to know that. But anyone who was Facebook or Snapchat friends with Brittany Masters would have seen the stuff about Riley. Would people here end up making fun of her, too? Or be sugary kind to her out of pity? Maybe they'd act nice to her face, then talk behind her back.

Even Morgan—was all this niceness real?

After all Riley had lived through, she didn't really know who to trust. Other than her mother. And now Mr. Larrett.

By the time Riley and her mom got in the car, the two mothers had a schedule worked out for driving to and from school. Riley's mom would bring them, and Morgan's would pick them up. Morgan seemed happy with that idea. Riley was, too. She waved goodbye as they drove out of the school parking lot.

Riley was so close to having new real friends. This *had* to work. *Please, God.*

One thing was for sure. She'd do anything to make that happen, and to make everyone *keep* liking her.

Anything.

THURSDAY, NOVEMBER 16

CHAPTER 17

P AYTON — The Kootenai County Sheriff's Office is searching for a woman who failed to return home Tuesday night, and whose car was found abandoned on Shelkins Road Wednesday morning.

The Sheriff's Office was informed that Paula Tellinger was last seen leaving the downtown office of Jack Larrett Financial on Corbin Street around 4:30 p.m. Tuesday. Tellinger's roommate, Linda Gladstone, told law enforcement Tellinger left their shared home that afternoon to go to an unscheduled meeting with Jack Larrett, saying she would be home afterward. Gladstone reported that Tellinger looked angry as she left but did not explain why.

At 6 a.m. Wednesday the Sheriff's Office responded to a report of an abandoned vehicle on Shelkins Road. A run of the plates revealed the car belonged to Paula Tellinger. The car was towed to the county forensic lot for inspection. A source from the Sheriff's Office told *The CDA Press* that a dusting for fingerprints yielded very few usable prints.

Friends who were questioned say they do not know where Tellinger is and have no knowledge of her planning to leave the area.

Anyone with information is urged to call the Sheriff's Office at 208-446-1300. Law enforcement are interested in talking to anyone who may have seen Tellinger between 4:30 Tuesday afternoon and 6 a.m. Wednesday, when her car was found.

Tellinger is white, 43 years old, 5-foot-3 and 115 pounds, with blonde hair and brown eyes. She was last seen wearing jeans and boots, a red sweater, and had a white scarf wrapped around her head.

A red sweater.
The word burned into my brain. *Red.*

I smacked the morning paper down on my desk.

Who knew to tell law enforcement she was wearing red? I racked my mind until the obvious answer bounced to the surface. Paula's roommate, Linda. She'd seen Paula leave their house. Of course she knew what Paula had been wearing.

I bent over my desk, feeling sick. How stupid were we? Why did J.L. think my wearing Paula's white scarf was enough to hide my identity? Even if video camera pictures of my face were grainy, my sweater was the wrong color. Law enforcement would see the blue sweater, and they'd figure it out. Because Paula walked *in this door wearing red.*

My stomach turned over. I shoved away from my desk, ran to the bathroom, and threw up.

When I was done I sat on the closed toilet lid, doubled over, staring at the tile floor until it blurred. If I'd been tired from lack of sleep the previous day, by Thursday I was twice as bad. I'd tossed and turned all night.

How long would it be before some Sheriff's deputy—maybe Eric—came for me?

I hated J.L.

But how Riley's life had changed. She'd spent hours the night before texting with Morgan and other girls in her Hayden Prep class. Riley showed me all her new Facebook friends, the welcoming updates they'd written on her page. This morning I'd taken her and Morgan to school, listening to their chatter about teachers and students. Riley was a completely different kid. All because of J.L.

Well, he had me where he wanted.

I heard the front door of the office open and close. J.L. had arrived. I pushed to my feet and took a few deep breaths before stepping out of the bathroom.

J.L. took one look at my face and stilled. "You all right?"

"I'm fine." I headed for my desk.

He watched me pull out my chair. "Riley and Morgan get off to school okay?"

"Yes. That's going great." My words fell like lead. I picked up the newspaper and thrust it toward him. "Read this."

He held my gaze as he accepted the paper. Then scanned the article and handed it back to me. "All sounds about right."

. How could he be so *calm?* "It says *red sweater*. They know she was wearing red!"

"You think they wouldn't know?"

"*You* told me no one would remember!"

"Okay, so they did. I'm not surprised. Somebody was bound to see her on her way here. It's why we didn't deny she was here in the first place."

"But you *told* me—"

"I told you that just to keep you calm. And look at you now."

Like I shouldn't be upset?

He shrugged. "If you're worried about video coverage, it won't matter. It was getting dark, Cara. Bright red, bright blue—they look the same in the dark. They won't be able to tell. What they *will* see is the white scarf. White stands out."

"Why didn't you tell me that before?"

"What difference does it make?"

I pressed my fingers into the paper. What he said did make sense. Colors were hard to discern in the dark. But how had J.L. thought of this fact so quickly, as Paula's body lay at his feet?

J.L. pointed at me. "I'm telling you—*stop worrying*. It won't do any good. If anything, it will just trip you up somewhere. And that we can't afford. So just do your job here. And be thankful that life has suddenly gotten so much better for your daughter."

Anger flashed white-hot in my chest. I wanted to scream at him. *That's why you paid for her school, isn't it! You just want to keep me quiet!* I felt the words form in the back of my throat, rise up to my tongue. My mouth opened. J.L. watched me, surely seeing the disgust on my face, the disloyal thoughts in my eyes. The moment hung in the air—and I knew the choice I made in the next second would set my course. It was now or never. Stand up to him, try to regain what was left of my self-worth—or not.

I wanted my life back. I wanted *me* back.

But what would be left of *me,* my life, if the Sheriff's Office found out? What would be left of Riley?

I snapped my mouth closed. Looked away.

Slowly, I loosened my fingers from the newspaper. Laid it with utmost care on my desk. Sat down.

I knew J.L. could see the beat of my heart.

On the right side of my desk sat the appointment book. I slid it in front of me and opened it.

"Today you have a meeting at 10:00 with Mrs. Honeycutt." My voice sounded like thin steel. "At 1:30 the Brewsters are coming in. At 3:30 you have a dentist check-up."

I raised my eyes to J.L. "I will continue working on the tax packets. I should be able to mail them this afternoon."

J.L. nodded. He gave me a long, assessing look, then laid a hand across the back of his neck and gazed out the window.

"Tell me about Riley," he said. "She's happier now, isn't she? I know she and Morgan talked a lot last night. I know Morgan stayed at school yesterday to meet both of you."

And *I* knew what J.L. was doing. "Yes, she's happy. Morgan was very kind to her."

J.L.'s lips curved. "Good. It worked, then."

What a loaded sentence. "Yes. It worked."

"Great." J.L. shifted his weight, placing his hands on his hips. "You know my first wife couldn't have children?"

The sudden change in subject stopped me. "No, I didn't."

"Yeah. She ... we tried for a long time before giving up. But I so wanted kids. She did, too. That marriage fell apart after twenty-three years. Then I met Rachelle two years later. We got married, and she had Morgan the following year. I was fifty." J.L. shook his head. "Fifty years old, and a dad for the first time, imagine that. I was over the moon. We would have had more, but about the time we'd have tried again we almost lost Morgan."

"Lost her?"

"Bacterial meningitis. She was nine. She was sick a long time. At death's door. I thought ..." J.L. looked away. "I thought I would go mad. I *couldn't* lose her. She's my everything. I'd waited so long to have her."

That, I understood. A parent's desperate love for a child.

"She finally got better. And today she has no repercussions, which is a miracle in itself. She could have suffered brain damage, hearing loss, or had some kind of learning disability. But—no." J.L. took a deep breath. "That's why, today, I'd do anything to protect her. And why I'm so ... I don't know, tuned in to other people's kids. People around town. Eric's. Yours. I'll do anything to help a kid. For the kid's sake—after I watched how Morgan suffered. And for the parents' sake. Because I know how *I* suffered."

J.L.'s mouth hung open, then closed, as if he'd run out of words.

I averted my eyes, searching for a response. Half of me felt guilty for thinking what he'd done for Riley was pure manipulation.

"I'm so sorry. I didn't know."

"Yeah. Well." He gestured with one hand. "Anyway, if you hear anything bad from Riley, something at school she's not happy about—let me know. I'll see if I can fix it."

Fix it. Was that what J.L. was trying to do? Help me all he could after wrecking my life? Maybe he wasn't trying to control every part of me. Maybe this was penance. And he truly wanted to help.

Inside me a small bloom of hope unfolded. If I could just keep our secret, not be found out—my future need not be forever ruined. I had to get over my guilt. Claw my way to a new normalcy.

I know that sounds callous. Where was the justice for Paula? But once again it all came down to my daughter. I had to make this work for Riley.

Wouldn't you do the same for your child?

"J.L." I managed a little smile. "Thank you. I mean that."

He dipped his chin in a nod and walked into his office, shutting the door behind him.

CHAPTER 18

Riley quickly saw that Hayden Prep was nothing like Payton Middle School. First, it was a lot smaller, even though it included kindergarten through high school. There were only fourteen students in eighth grade, like Morgan had said. Plus, grades eight and up were in a different wing of the building from the younger students, so middle through twelve kind of felt like its own world.

But the most important thing—Riley had friends. Morgan was so nice Riley could hardly believe it. And Morgan's clothes! They were amazing. Everything was designer, including her Coach purse. Today she wore a brown leather jacket over a soft-looking white sweater and jeans. Brown boots with a Michael Kors logo on the side. Riley looked shabby next to her, even after choosing the best clothes she had this morning. But Morgan didn't seem to notice. At least she didn't say so. And because *she* accepted Riley so quickly, everyone else did, too. Morgan's closest friends in their grade were Alissa, who had gorgeous blonde hair and danced in the hallway; Lauren, who talked really fast and was so funny; and Bella, who was about the same size—maybe even bigger—as Riley. *That* really made her feel good.

There was another girl who sometimes hung around Morgan and her group but wasn't really a part of it. Morgan wasn't mean to her or anything. She just … didn't pay her much attention. The girl's name was Claire. She wasn't as pretty as the other four, with short dark hair and glasses. She had this cool, removed look, like she didn't really need anybody. Was that an act? Riley could understand the hurt of being left out. Claire's attitude could just be a way of protecting herself. She and Claire talked a little between classes. Turned out their lockers were next to each other. Claire was nice and obviously real smart. She had a way of talking that sounded older than most eighth graders.

As for the classes at Hayden Prep, they were harder. In math they were doing algebra beyond what Riley had studied before. She'd have some catching up to do. And in geography they had a test next week on *four* chapters. That was a lot at once.

"It's okay, we'll study together," Morgan said as they entered the classroom for third period—history. Lauren, Bella, and Alissa were right behind them.

Lauren put her hands up in a *don't shoot me* gesture. She was like that—over-dramatic. "It's just memorizing anyway, long enough to remember for the test. Then you can forget it."

Morgan rolled her eyes. "You're not supposed to forget it, Lor. That's what education is all about."

"It's *geography*. What do I care what they eat in Madagascar?"

"Madagascar! We're studying India, you dummy."

"Isn't that where Madagascar is?"

Morgan looked at Riley and shook her head. "See why you *need* geography?"

"Yeah." Riley laughed. But truth was, she had no idea where Madagascar was, either.

Morgan chose a seat first, and Alissa sat across from her. "Riley, you can sit here." Morgan pointed to the seat behind her. Bella chose the chair across from Riley. Lauren plopped down behind Bella. Claire took the seat behind Lauren.

"What's this teacher like?" Riley whispered to Bella.

Bella opened her mouth to answer, but Morgan swiveled around and cut in. "Mrs. Langston. She's hard but good. We like her."

Alissa turned around in her chair, tossing bangs out of her eyes. She and Bella nodded.

"She's got a little girl I babysit for sometimes," Lauren said. "She's four and so cute."

Babysitting for a teacher? Riley wiggled sideways in her seat so she could see Lauren behind her. "Isn't that kind of weird, being in her house?"

"Not at all. It's not like that here. I mean, everybody's real close."

That sounded good. Right? As long as Riley stayed in the middle of that closeness.

Riley's gaze strayed to a boy three rows over. She'd met him this morning in first class. Well, she'd met everybody in her grade. But *him* … His name was Grant. He had dark hair in a buzz cut and hazel eyes. So hot.

Morgan turned her head to see who Riley was looking at. She swung back around and raised her eyebrows. "You like him?" She kept her voice low.

"I … no."

"Yes you do."

"I don't even know him."

"So I'll tell you. He's new this year. Used to go to public school. Lives in Coeur d'Alene. He's quiet." Morgan gave a dismissive shrug.

"You don't like him?" Riley asked.

Morgan flipped her hand in the air. "I've tried talking to him, he just doesn't have much to say. Boring, if you ask me."

Lauren, Alissa, and Bella moved their eyes from Morgan to Riley and back. Behind Lauren, Claire was listening to everything, not saying a word. She, too, looked from Morgan to Riley. There was something on their faces, like acknowledgment of a fact they'd never say. Did Morgan not like Grant just because he wouldn't respond to her? Because she seemed to be the leader of just about everybody else. Riley was already getting the impression Morgan was used to having her way.

"Hey, Riley." Alissa made a point of changing the subject. "You coming to the party on Saturday?"

"What party?"

"Oh, yeah," Morgan said, "you should totally come. It's at Brandon's house."

"Who's Brandon?"

"He's in ninth grade. Really hot. He goes out with Taryn, also in ninth. You'll meet 'em at lunch today. Anyway, we'll all be there. Tell your mom about it. Starts at 7:00. We could pick you up. He lives in Hayden."

A party. Fear and excitement whirled in Riley's stomach. Of course she wanted to go. But what if everybody there didn't like her? What if this all fell apart, and somebody got mad at her for some little thing? She'd be stuck at a party with no way out. Having to call her mom to come get her like some little kid.

Morgan was watching Riley. "What? Don't you want to go?"

Her tone said Riley needed to say yes. Like you didn't say no to an invitation from Morgan. Bella and Lauren were leaning toward Riley, waiting for her answer.

"Of course I want to go!" Riley smiled. "I was just wondering if my mom will let me. She doesn't know who Brandon is."

"She knows *me*." Morgan pointed to her chest. "And that's what counts, right? My dad's her boss. He'll tell her to let you go."

Would he do that? It wasn't like Mr. Larrett was boss of her mom's personal life. But—he *was* the one who'd paid Riley's tuition. *Did* Morgan know that?

"I'll ask, okay?" Riley said. "I really wanna come."

Would Grant be there? Riley didn't want to ask. And was Claire invited? None of the other girls had even looked at her as they talked about the party. Which wasn't nice at all. Riley knew what it felt like to be left out. She should ask Morgan right now if Claire was coming. Claire would hear, and how could Morgan say a flat out no in front of her?

Riley's mouth opened, but no words came. What if Morgan didn't like being pushed into a corner like that? What if she got mad?

Riley closed her lips. She stole a glance back at Claire, and for a second their eyes met. Claire firmed her mouth, like she knew what Riley was thinking. Guilt streaked through Riley. She looked away.

The bell rang. Up front, Mrs. Langston moved in front of her desk. "All right, class, everyone looking up here."

"You'll be there, don't worry," Morgan whispered. "I'll make sure." She gave Riley a wink and turned around to face the teacher.

CHAPTER 19

At noon I headed home, longing for one hour by myself in the house. One hour away from … everything. I made a sandwich and ate it by rote at the kitchen table, barely tasting it. When I was almost finished, my cell rang.

Riley.

The old fear shot through me. I snatched up the phone. "Riley, you okay?"

"Yeah! Everything's going really good."

My eyes closed in relief. "How are—"

"I just wanted to ask you something because I don't have much time at lunch. You know Paula Tellinger?"

The name glued me to my chair. "Why?"

"'Cause I met this girl in ninth grade—her name is April—and she told me she heard my mom worked for Morgan's dad, and that this woman, Paula Tellinger, is missing. And she was in J.L.'s office before she disappeared. Paula, I mean. April said it was in the paper."

"Oh. Yes, that's true."

"Wow. So—is she still missing?"

"Apparently so."

"Did the cops talk to you about it?"

I licked my lips. "Deputy, you mean. Yes."

"They talked to *you*? Really? Just like those crime shows on TV?" Morbid fascination laced Riley's tone.

"Riley, this isn't a show. This is real life. And this is a *real* person who's missing."

"I know." She paused, as if to convince me of her contrition. "So where is she?"

"How should I know?"

"Well, what did she say to you? 'Cause I heard right after she left your office she just ... left town. They found her car."

Not until that moment had I even thought about Riley hearing gossip regarding Paula's disappearance. Stupid, I know. But between her own issues and mine, I'd had no time to consider this conversation.

"First of all, Riley, be careful about believing everything you hear. Some things may be true. But then rumors start flying around, and false stuff gets mixed in with the truth. That doesn't help anybody."

"I know. But it was in the paper, April told me. I asked Morgan about it, but she kinda shrugged and said lots of people go to her dad's office. I just wondered if Paula said anything to you. Like, you know, if you could give the police a clue. Or deputy, whoever."

My heart sank. I focused on a plastic food container sitting on the counter. The remainder of the cookies Riley had baked two days ago sat inside. *"I'm going to be a baker when I grow up ..."*

I'd always promised my daughter I'd never lie to her. Now that was exactly what I was doing.

"Riley, I don't know anything. She came to the office to talk to J.L. They went into his personal office together and closed the door. Later—she left. That's it. I don't know where she went or what she did."

Did my words sound too tight? Defensive?

"Oh. Okay."

How easily my daughter believed me. Pain shot through my lungs.

"Well, if the deputy comes back to talk to you, will you tell me?"

"Why?"

"Because I want to know! April said people don't just disappear from Payton. And she heard from her cousin that Paula 'hung around with the wrong crowd.' Those exact words. And that maybe Paula was murdered."

I shuddered. "That's just what I'm talking about, Riley." Now my voice *was* off—too sharp. I couldn't help it. "That's just rumor, and I don't want you spreading it. This Paula probably has family in the area. You want them hearing that? These are *people* we're talking about. Real people's lives."

Yes, Cara. Real people's lives.

"Okay, Mom, okay!" Riley huffed. "I just wanted to know, is all. You don't have to get mad."

I took a deep breath. "I'm not mad. I'm just … late, actually. I'm at lunch now and need to get back to the office. Call me after school, all right?"

"Yeah. I will. Bye."

I clicked off the call and pushed my plate away. Then hunched low over the table, feeling the heat of my breath against the wood. I'd come home for an hour's peace alone—and now look at me. Why did I think I could go *anywhere* and find peace? My entire life was tainted. Weighted with a burden I didn't know how to bear. Now I was even lying to the very person I wanted to protect. I didn't deserve peace.

CHAPTER 20

I returned to work at 1:00, my sandwich sitting heavily in my stomach. It took all my mental energy to get back to the task at hand—sealing and addressing J.L.'s tax preparation packets. I was almost done. What else to do but try to drown my thoughts in work?

At 1:30, just after I'd finished the job, the Brewsters arrived for their appointment. I'd made sure there was fresh coffee to serve them. And, of course, to serve J.L. The man drank coffee all day. You'd think his nerves would jitter right out of his body.

The packets sat in three large boxes, ready to be taken to the post office, two blocks down Corbin. Preparing all those packet labels had provided my first look at J.L.'s complete list of clients. Some of the names stood out. Such as Anthony Rainwell, the county sheriff. And Eric Chandler.

The Brewsters looked to be in their late sixties. She had a stylish short cut of gray hair. His face was long and friendly.

"Well, hello there." Mrs. Brewster extended a hand toward me. "You must be J.L.'s new gal."

"Don't call her a gal, that's sexist." Mr. Brewster shook his head at me, as if to say *sorry*.

His wife gave a little huff. "It's not sexist, I'm a gal, too." She shook her head at me, too, as if to say—*men*. "And gals are a lot smarter than guys, so there you go."

I stood to greet them. "Nice to meet you, I'm Cara."

"Nice to meet you, too," they said in stereo.

Clearly these two had been married a long time. They seemed in perfect sync with each other. Sudden loneliness shot through me. I so wanted that. A strong marriage that would last for years. Love built on trust and respect. After my divorce, I'd dared to dream I would find that someday. But now trust was something I could never truly have. I would forever harbor a terrible secret. How do you build a relationship on a lie?

That's the problem with hidden sin. *You* know. It affects what you do, how you act. And God knows.

Mrs. Brewster slid off her coat. "You new in town? I think I heard that somewhere."

People were talking about *me*? "Yes. Brand new. I moved here and started working right away."

"Well, that's great. I'm sure it'll be a wonderful job for you. And it's good to see J.L. managed to replace Edith in such a short time. So sad about her."

Sad? A tingle ran through my veins. J.L. had mentioned the name *Edith* when he interviewed me. That she'd been with him for over ten years. But I'd never asked why she left the job.

"Here, let me take your coat." Did my voice sound normal? "Mr. Brewster, shall I take yours, too?" I hung them both up on the antler tree.

"What happened to Edith?" I returned to my desk.

"Oh, you didn't know?" Mrs. Brewster ran a hand through her hair. "She died suddenly, poor thing. Right here in the office. She was only sixty-three. Apparently a heart attack. But she'd been so fit up to then. Exercising and healthy. It was a real shock to everyone."

My face muscles froze. "Oh. I had no idea."

"Yes, well. The last time I talked to Edith—"

J.L.'s door opened. "Well, hello there, Mike and Jessie." His voice boomed, so unconcerned. So friendly. As if the ceiling hadn't just crashed down around me. He strode over to shake the Brewsters' hands. "I see you've met Cara."

"Yes." Mike Brewster smiled at me. "Glad to see you've found a new assistant."

So soon after Edith's death.

I watched J.L.'s face. Not a flinch, no hint of anything amiss. "Yes, indeed. Well, come on in." He gestured toward his office. "Do either of you want coffee?"

"No, thanks." Again, in stereo.

"All right, then. Cara, please bring up their investments for me."

"Okay." My legs felt rubbery. I needed to get out of there. Needed to *think.* "These are ready to go to the post office." I pointed to the boxes. "I'll go ahead and take them over while you're meeting."

"Fine."

J.L. ushered the clients into his office and closed the door.

I shut my eyes and dragged in a breath. Returned to my desk and sat down hard.

Stay calm, Cara. This was nothing. Right? Edith had a heart attack out of the blue. It happens.

I shoved my suspicions aside.

On auto-pilot, I brought up the Brewsters' file so they could review their portfolio with J.L. on his monitor. I couldn't help seeing the bottom line of their accounts. Okay, I looked for it. Over three million dollars.

Wow. Maybe that's why they were so happy. Maybe it wasn't their relationship at all.

Crazy, the things you tell yourself just to stay sane.

That done, I clicked on the Internet to Google Edith—then stopped. Not here, on this computer.

I slid on my coat and one by one carried the heavy boxes of tax packets to my car, loading two in the trunk and one in the backseat. The morning was clear and cold. I drove to the post office, parked and pulled out my phone. At Google I typed in *Edith Payton Idaho Larrett Financial.* A *Coeur d'Alene Press* article appeared at the top: "Medics called to Larrett Financial."

I scanned the paragraphs, my mouth dry.

Her full name was Edith Brell. She'd died just six weeks ago, three weeks before my phone interview with J.L. *Six weeks.* He'd hired me immediately after that interview, and within seven days I'd moved to Payton. I began working for him Monday, November sixth. It had all happened so fast.

So had her death. Edith had left home "feeling fine," according to a neighbor who saw her leave for work. That afternoon she apparently collapsed at her desk. J.L. called 911. She was pronounced dead at the scene.

I dropped the phone in my lap and stared out the car window. Over ten years she'd worked for J.L. And he'd *barely mentioned her.* Why? And, come to think of it, why had he posted the job online? He knew so many people in this area. Surely someone knew someone who needed a job. Yet he'd brought me in, a stranger.

Did he kill Edith?

Breath caught in my throat.

No. Couldn't be. How could he have gotten away with it? A medical examiner would have declared the cause of death. If she'd been strangled, that would have been apparent. They must have done an autopsy, seen a damaged heart. A ticking time bomb that had suddenly blown.

But this was J.L., the man no one questioned.

What if Edith had found out something he was doing? And he had to get rid of her?

I pressed back against the seat, fixated on that thought. The idea grew prickly spikes that stuck in my brain.

Picking up my phone, I clicked through a few more Google hits. No follow-up article on Edith's death. Just an obituary. She left behind two children and five grandchildren, all of whom lived in this area. No mention of a husband.

Maybe it was better if J.L. *had* killed Edith. Because then he wouldn't dare kill me. Two assistants, both suddenly dead in his office? That was too coincidental, even for him.

I squeezed my eyes shut. How could I even think such a horrible thing?

Unless, of course, he dumped my body over a cliff.

Stop it, Cara. I shook my head. Threw the phone in my purse.

I shoved all scenarios to one corner of my mind and got out of the car. Focused on carrying the box from the backseat into the post office. I dropped it into a corner, out of the way, and turned to bring in the second. As I neared the door a woman stopped me. Maybe mid-fifties, with straggly brown hair and weathered skin. "You got more?" she asked. "I'll help ya." A no-nonsense air emanated from her, as if she'd lived a hard life and knew how to get by.

"Oh, thanks, no need."

She flapped a hand in the air, like swatting a fly. "No bother. Come on, I'll help."

I managed a smile. "Thanks."

"The boxes are for J.L. aren't they?" the woman asked as we stepped outside. "I'm Margie Stohl, by the way. I seen you goin' in and out of his building."

The words jagged through me. Going in and out—*when?*

We reached my car. "I'm Cara." I opened the trunk. "You work near J.L.'s building?"

"Across the street. At the dry cleaners."

That was near where Paula's car had been parked.

I picked up a box and handed it to Margie. Pulled out the last one and balanced it awkwardly against the bumper as I closed the trunk.

"I read in the paper about Paula." Margie faced me, squinting into the sun. "So awful. Wonder what's happened to her."

"We wonder, too."

"Yeah. She's a friend a mine. But she didn't say anything about takin' off like that. I think somethin' bad happened to her." Margie held my gaze, waiting. It struck me that she was out for information.

"Really? I heard that she was kind of ..." *Careful, Cara. Just plant an idea.* "I heard she recently broke up with someone, and maybe she wanted to get out of town."

Margie wagged her head. "That's true. But I doubt it. She wanted Vince back in the worst way. So I still say somethin' bad's happened."

"Like what?"

Margie raised a shoulder. "Who knows. I seen her that day, you know, goin' into your building. I looked up some time later and seen her car drivin' away. I noticed that white scarf on her head, like the newspaper said. That's the last I seen of her."

The scarf. That saving detail.

Red sweater. The sudden thought dropped a stone in my lungs. "Oh. Uh-huh. Did you happen to see what she was wearing?"

Margie gave me a long look. "Just the scarf. She was driving away."

I managed a nod. "Did you tell the Sheriff's deputy about the scarf?"

"Yup. Couldn't a been that much help, you probably told 'em the same thing."

I nodded again. She'd likely also told them her premonition of "somethin' bad." Was that the sense of this whole town? Eric Chandler's words echoed in my head: *It just doesn't look right.*

I was cold, and the box was heavy. I started walking toward the post office door. Margie followed. Inside we stacked the three boxes on top of one another. Two people stood in line ahead of me.

"Thanks for your help." I smiled at Margie.

"No problem." She looked me in the eye. "Take care a yourself, now." She turned toward the door, throwing back over her shoulder, "Be careful workin' for J.L."

"What?" My too-sharp response stopped her. "What do you mean?"

"Ah, nothin'." She waved her hand. "He's just a workaholic, that's all. Worked Edith right into a heart attack. 'Course you're a lot younger, so ..." Margie shrugged and walked away.

I stared after her, pulse skipping. *Be careful ... heart attack.* Is that really all she'd meant?

The line ahead of me moved. I stepped forward.

Of course that's all she meant. Margie was just a gossip. Working at the dry cleaners all those years, seeing people come in and out—she probably knew everyone in town. What they wore and the stains they got on their clothes—which could tell her a lot. Hadn't she helped me only to hear what I knew about Paula Tellinger?

This was a small town, with most people knowing one other. There would be plenty gossips around. If the tiniest suspicion of me or J.L. arose, it would be all over Payton in no time. Including right to my own daughter's ears.

Renewed fear for Riley flashed through me. She could never hear such rumors. I had to continue to do everything I could to deflect suspicion away from J.L. and me. *Everything*.

No matter the cost to my own soul.

Eric Chandler
Paula Tellinger Disappearance—Questions
2 p.m., 11/16

P's car parked 320 Corbin—witness Margie Stohl.
Security camera 500 Corbin—no sighting of car.
Turned at 400 block? Camera 400 & Trent—no car. ??

Linda Gladstone—P. wearing red sweater. Margie
Stohl—blue sweater. ??

CHAPTER 21

When I returned to the office, the Brewsters' coats still hung on the antler tree. Their meeting with J.L. wasn't over.

The day's mail sat on my desk, delivered while I'd been out. I reached for the top envelope—and my cell phone rang.

Riley.

She had one more hour of her first day at Hayden Prep but couldn't wait to tell me how "totally great" the day had gone, and about all her new friends. Plus, Morgan had invited Riley to her house for the afternoon. I could pick her up from there when I got off work.

"Okay, Mom? *Please?*" Riley's tone was breathy, excited.

Now my daughter would be at J.L.'s *house*. "What about your homework?"

"We're gonna study together. I'll get it done."

If I said no, how would that look to Morgan and her mother? To J.L.?

"Mom!"

"Okay. But your homework better be done. If this ends up getting in the way of doing your work, I won't say yes next time."

"Deal, bye!" Riley clicked off before I could change my mind. Dark thoughts filled me. Riley at J.L.'s house. And I'd have to go there to pick her up. Talk to Rachelle again. She'd been very gracious yesterday, but she was J.L.'s wife. All this sudden closeness between his family and mine ...

Be careful workin' for J.L.

His office door opened. He and the Brewsters appeared, laughing and talking about their grandchildren. The youngest, I gathered, was Grace, who would graduate in May from Gonzaga in Spokane. "Years ago J.L. helped us set up trust accounts for the grandkids' college," Mrs. Brewster told me. "How grateful we all are for that. The investments have paid off wonderfully, and not one of those kids graduated owing loan payments." She beamed at J.L.

Of course he'd helped their grandchildren. Saint J.L.

I pulled the Brewsters' coats off the antler tree and held each one out for them to slip on. "See you again in six months, dear." Jessie Brewster buttoned her coat. "Keep warm! Snow will be here soon."

J.L. and I bid them goodbye. As I closed the door, I turned to see him sifting through the mail on my desk.

"Nothing here but the usual bills." He tossed down an envelope and regarded me.

A strained moment passed.

J.L. stuck his right hand in his pocket, jingling coins. "I heard them talking about Edith when I came out."

I gave a little shrug.

"She was a wonderful woman. Edith. With me a long time."

"So I heard."

Why hadn't he told me about her? Did he really think I wouldn't learn of her death from someone in town?

J.L. probed me with another long look. He gestured toward my desk. "She died of a sudden heart attack. Right here. I was in my office with the door closed. When I came out she was ..." Pain twinged across J.L.'s forehead. "She was slumped over the desk, almost like she was sleeping. I said some remark like 'Edith, you need a nap?' Expecting her to push up and be embarrassed, you know." J.L. cleared his throat. "But she didn't move."

Sadness radiated from him. Was it real?

"What did you do?"

"Tried to revive her. But it was clear she'd been there awhile. I called 911. They came in a hurry. They worked on her, but they knew. *I* knew. They pronounced her dead before they even carried her away." J.L. gazed out the window, memories of the scene playing across his face. "They left with her, and I just ... sat down in her chair and cried like a baby. All I could think of was—I was *here.* Just on the other side of that door. Working away, concentrating hard like I do. If I'd just been a little more attentive—would I have heard something? Because there was no doubt in my mind I could have saved her if I'd found her earlier."

J.L.'s words ran out. The hand in his pocket jingled coins again.

"I'm so sorry." My words fell quietly, no accusation in them. At the moment J.L. seemed so ... real. Vulnerable, like the rest of us.

Then I thought of Paula Tellinger, strangled and sprawled on his office floor.

Who *was* this man?

My eyes filled with unexpected tears. J.L. likely thought they were for him and Edith.

"How did they know it was a heart attack, J.L.?"

"Autopsy." He pulled a tissue from the holder on my desk and handed it to me. "She'd been so healthy. No one could have known the blockage was there."

I believed him. I chose to believe. Surely he couldn't have paid off the county medical examiner, not to mention the paramedics at the scene.

I wiped away my tears. "Why did you hire me? A stranger from Seattle. Why not someone in town?"

He considered the floor. "Edith had been with me for so long and was completely trustworthy. When I hired her, she was new to town, too. After she was gone, I didn't know anyone else in Payton who I'd want in this position. Like I told you in our interview, this job requires total discretion. You see the tax and investment accounts of people who live right here. I want someone learning the job first, then meeting people in town, rather than the other way around. I *don't* need some new assistant snooping into accounts to see how much their neighbor or best friend is worth."

Could I believe this?

"You're capable, Cara. I liked you. And you clearly needed a new start."

I'd also needed a man who wouldn't victimize me—for the first time in my life.

"I'm sorry." J.L. spread his hands. "I never meant for ... this to happen. You know that."

"Yes." I looked away.

J.L. drew up straight. "Well, I got a dentist appointment to get to. I'll be going home from there, so see you tomorrow." He headed for the door. "I trust Riley had a good day at school?"

"She did. Thank you so much."

He nodded. "Good. Very good. Makes it ..."

All worthwhile? That's a statement he couldn't finish. Still, I knew what he'd done. He'd planted the thought in my brain.

"See you tomorrow, Cara."

As the door closed behind J.L., I lingered in the middle of the room, gazing at the antler coat tree. Which made me think of hunting. Then of the Coeur d'Alene National Forest, where Paula's body lay, crumpled and broken, at the bottom of that cliff. Were her eyes still open? Staring up at the cold, unrelenting sky?

A shudder shook me. I rubbed my arms, forcing it away. Dwelling on these dark memories would do me no good. I needed to look forward.

I returned to my desk, seeking escape in work.

Two minutes later the phone rang. Deputy Eric Chandler.

Again? Was this guy Payton's own Columbo?

I clutched the receiver, heart revving. One thing about Columbo—he always won.

CHAPTER 22

Morgan's house was amazing. Riley had already seen the outside of it when she and her mom picked up Morgan for school that morning. But the inside looked even better. It was really big, with lots of warm-looking wood and a great room with a thirty-foot ceiling. It was in the forest on four acres, Morgan said. With beautiful trees and a path through the woods, and even a creek. Morgan's parents' room was on the first floor. Hers was on the second—the biggest bedroom Riley had ever seen. It was painted in pale blue and white. A thick, fluffy bedspread and lots of pillows on a king-sized bed. Matching curtains on a *lot* of windows.

"Why do you have such a big bed?" Riley gaped at it.

"There's plenty of space for it." Morgan shrugged. "And lots of girls can be on it for a sleepover."

How cool it must be to have friends sleep over at your house. Riley had never experienced that. No way could it happen when she'd lived with her dad. She'd never had a friend over *at all*, because—who knew what that friend might see her dad do? And now her room in Payton was so small, with just a twin bed. No space for a second person.

"Does your mom work?" Riley asked. Rachelle—Riley was allowed to call her that—was downstairs in the kitchen, making brownies.

"No. Doesn't have to. My dad makes all the money."

Morgan said it casually, like it was nothing. She'd probably never wanted anything she didn't get.

Jealousy panged through Riley.

"Wanna see my closet?" Morgan led Riley through a door into a huge walk-in room, with racks of hanging clothes and a bunch of dressers.

"Wow." Riley did a slow circle. "Looks like you never need to buy anything to wear ever again."

Morgan laughed. "You can never have too many clothes!"

What a fairyland. People really lived like this? While her own life, and her mom's life, had been so hard?

"You look kinda stunned, Riley." Morgan laughed again.

Was she laughing at her?

"No, it's just … a lot. I mean, I don't have a house like this."

"I know."

And still she'd treated Riley nothing but nice at school.

They left the closet, Morgan closing the door behind them.

"Does your dad give you whatever you want?" Riley's gaze landed on Morgan's dresser, full of framed pictures of their family.

"Yeah. As long as I get good grades. Which I do. How about your mom?"

That was a laugh. Although Riley had no doubt her mom *wanted* to give her more. "She doesn't … we can't afford it. I don't …" Riley hesitated. This was unknown territory with Morgan. "I don't have a dad. I mean I do, but he's not around. And he doesn't pay for anything. So it's just my mom working."

For Morgan's dad. The thought hung in the air.

"I'm sorry." Morgan rubbed Riley's arm. "Losing a dad can't be easy."

Riley pressed her lips together. "Doesn't matter."

Morgan gazed at Riley, like she knew it did.

Riley drew a breath. "We need to do homework. I promised my mom I'd get it done."

"Yeah."

They'd dropped their backpacks near the doorway. Morgan and Riley picked them up, tossing them on the bed. Morgan shut the door to her room, then climbed onto the middle of the bed, sitting cross-legged. "Here." She patted the comforter beside her.

Riley sat.

"Let's do math first." Morgan pulled out the textbook.

Riley's heart sank. Right off she'd show Morgan how behind she was. She didn't understand any of what they'd talked about in class. "Okay."

But Morgan turned out to be a really good tutor. And she totally understood about Riley being behind. "Most kids are when they come to Hayden Prep from a public school. You'll catch up soon enough." She explained to Riley the logic processes in the algebra problems—and she began to get it. That felt so good. She wasn't dumb, she just hadn't been taught right.

If she worked really hard, maybe she could make the best grades in class. Then everybody would look up to her.

"When your mom comes to pick you up we can tell her about the party on Saturday." Morgan threw out the comment as they put their math textbooks away.

Ask, Riley wanted to reply. She asked her mom to do things, she didn't *tell* her. But Riley said nothing.

Morgan leaned toward Riley, her voice dropping. "I have a—"

A knock sounded on Morgan's door. She snapped her mouth shut. The door opened, and her mom came in, carrying two plates of brownies and some napkins.

"Wow, these look great." Riley accepted her plate from Rachelle. "Thank you!"

"Hope you like them, girls." Rachelle left, shutting the door behind her.

Morgan picked up a brownie daintily between her thumb and forefinger. "So." She waved the brownie around. "I started to tell you I have a new boyfriend. Just met him last week."

"Yeah? At school?" Riley took her first bite. The brownie was warm and fabulous.

"Not at our school. At a public school. He's sixteen."

"Sixteen!"

"Yeah. Sophomore in high school. But you can't talk about it to anybody, especially your mom."

"I wouldn't tell my mom that." Riley took another bite. "Does your mom know?"

"No way. My dad would kill me. I'm not supposed to have a boyfriend until *I'm* sixteen." Morgan flicked a look at the ceiling. "So stupid."

Dating somebody three years older. Riley couldn't even imagine. Sixteen was so *mature.*

"Want to know something else?" Morgan leaned forward and lowered her voice. "You're the only person that knows."

Really? "Why?"

Morgan shrugged. "Just haven't told anybody else. I don't even want Alissa, Lauren, and Bella to know. Not yet. So keep this between me and you, okay?"

"Okay." Wow. Morgan was trusting *only* her with this. "When can you see him? I mean, if nobody knows …."

"Yeah, it's hard. But he told me he'll show up at the party Saturday. Not that he's invited—because no one else knows him. But the party will be in Brandon's basement—you know, one of those walk-out lower levels that has a door to the backyard? Blaze will come in that way."

"Blaze? His name is *Blaze*?"

"That's what everybody calls him. His real name is Aaron."

"Why do they call him that?"

Morgan lifted both shoulders. "I don't know. 'Cause he's hot!"

They laughed.

Riley's first brownie was gone. She picked up the second. "Won't Brandon's parents find out? Don't they come down and check on everybody?" Her mom sure would. She'd be down there every ten minutes. And she'd remember everyone who'd come through the front door.

"They'll check, but there's different rooms down there so … it'll work out."

"Brandon won't care?"

"No. He wants me at his parties! Else hardly anyone would come. Besides, I haven't told him Blaze is coming. It'll just be a surprise." Morgan wiped her fingers on her napkin. "There'll be more parties next month for Christmas. Can't wait! Think of it, Thanksgiving's just next week."

Riley nodded. She wanted to go to every party out there. She'd have to keep close to Morgan to do that. One day at Hayden Prep, and Riley saw how things were. Morgan pretty much ran the show. Good thing she was so nice.

But she wasn't nice to Claire. She totally ignored her, like Claire didn't exist. That had to hurt.

Clearly, you wouldn't want to get on Morgan's bad side.

CHAPTER 23

"Hi, Cara, how's your day going?" Eric Chandler's voice over the phone nearly stopped my heart.

"Fine." Multiple thoughts sped through my brain. *Play along. Don't panic. Get information.* "Did you find Paula Tellinger?"

"Afraid not. We're still looking."

I floundered for something else to say. A scene flashed before me—this man arresting me. Taking me to jail. How would he look at me then, with my soul tainted and laid bare? How could I ever sit in a jail cell, trapped, knowing my life was over? Riley's life would be over. They'd send her to her *father*. Or foster care.

"Is J.L. in?" Eric asked. "I have a quick question for him."

"He's at the dentist. Can I help?"

"Don't think so. Just wanted to ask a detail about his conversation with Paula."

What detail?

I swallowed. "I … went to the post office today and met Margie Stohl. The woman who works across the street at the dry cleaners?

She said she talked to you. That is, I guess it was you. She saw Paula drive away that day in her car."

"Yeah. We've got the timeline down, with your statement and Margie's. And a little while ago we looked at video from cameras going up Highway 95."

My fingers dug into the phone. "Did you see her car?"

"Yeah. Twice. Pictures are typically grainy on those things, but a white scarf on the driver's head makes it easier to spot a particular car."

"Oh." I could barely keep my voice from trembling. "I guess it would."

What did he mean? He said *driver*, not *Paula*. Was he baiting me?

The truth fell through my stomach like lead. Eric Chandler *knew*. He knew Paula was dead, and I'd moved her body. Now he was trying to trip me up. This call wasn't for J.L., it was for me. And once they had me in custody, J.L. would throw me under the bus. Completely. He'd have "no idea" that I'd killed Paula, or why.

"All right, Cara. I'll call J.L. later on his cell phone."

I don't remember saying goodbye to Eric Chandler. Or ending the call. My next memory has me back in the bathroom, throwing up.

Eventually I returned to my desk, drained and weak-kneed. I stared out the window like some zombie, knowing in a little over an hour I'd need to pick up Riley from J.L.'s house. I had to pull myself together.

What if tonight was my last night with her?

I closed my eyes and fought to breathe.

"Paula threatened me. She threatened my family." J.L.'s words seeped into my brain. Why would Paula threaten him? Was he lying about that? Even if she had made threats, J.L. didn't seem the

kind of man who'd be frightened of some crazy woman. He could have just called his BFF, the Sheriff. No need to kill Paula.

I thought that over, one finger tapping my desk.

What if she knew something about him? Something so powerful, so bad that its revelation would destroy him?

I'd had a similar thought about Edith.

What if they *both* found out the *same thing*? And J.L. really had killed Edith?

A shudder snaked down my back.

I stared at my computer, imagining scenarios. If they'd both found out the same thing, it must have something to do with J.L.'s work. Was he stealing from clients? Running some Ponzi scheme? But how would Paula discover that? She wasn't even a client.

But her ex-boyfriend, Vince Rayle, was.

What if she'd unearthed something about Vince's accounts? Something, apparently, *he* didn't even know. Maybe she came here threatening to expose J.L. to Vince. Maybe she'd demanded money. Tried to blackmail him.

That made sense. It felt right.

And I had to find out what it was.

If the Sheriff's Office came after me, if J.L. disavowed anything to do with Paula's murder, I'd need ammunition. Facts to convince them that he had a reason to kill her.

And I needed that ammunition now.

I jerked open the long drawer of my desk, searching for a jump drive to copy Vince's files. I'd take the drive home, study the information on my own computer. If J.L. found out, I'd be fired immediately. But I couldn't risk accessing the documents here, even with J.L. out of the office. Especially with him out of the office. He might notice the files had been accessed at a time he was gone.

No jump drive in the long drawer. I banged it shut and started on the three drawers on the side. *Please, please.*

Not one anywhere.

I heaved back in my chair with a sigh. Well, of course. The last thing J.L.'s assistant should have is a portable drive for copying confidential files.

Would he have one?

I shoved to my feet and headed for his office. The very air in that room seemed thicker. I glanced at the carpet where Paula had sprawled, her glazed eyes open and empty. Heart skidding, I opened J.L.'s top desk drawer and peered inside. No way could I move things around. He might notice. And if for some reason his dentist appointment was cancelled, and he walked in the door—I was doomed. Likely dead.

The first drawer held no luck. By then I was shaking. My body went hot, then cold as I continued to search.

Second drawer—nothing.

Or in the third.

I jerked up and thrust my hands in my hair. Now what?

My eyes fell on J.L.'s small wood cabinet against the wall. I hurried over and opened its doors. Saw three shelves. I snatched out boxes, examining their contents, making sure to put them back just as I'd found them.

On the bottom shelf—bingo. Four jump drives lay in a small box. None with a label. Unused?

I grabbed one and carefully replaced the box.

Back at my desk, I inserted the drive into my computer. Old documents came up, from 2013. *Please don't be full.*

Within two minutes I'd located all of Vince Rayle's files on my computer and dragged them to the portable drive. I sat trembling, watching the indicator move as each file was copied. My eyes jerked from the monitor to the front door. If J.L. walked through it …

On the third file the indicator stopped. An error message appeared. *Drive full.*

Air gushed from my mouth.

No turning back now. I ran into J.L.'s office and snatched up a second small drive. Pushed it into my computer and saw files from 2011 come up.

What if J.L. needed to access one of these old files for some reason? Surely they were mere back-ups—a secondary system in case the first back-ups were destroyed. Which meant it was doubtful he'd need them. But still … Somehow, some way I'd need to get these drives back in place tomorrow.

I dragged Vince Rayle's uncopied files over to the small drive. Then watched the progress again, rocking in my chair. It took forever.

They all copied.

I yanked out the jump drive and threw it, along with the first one, into the bottom of my purse. Laid my wallet on top of them. *Done.*

I collapsed against my chair and breathed, willing my pulse to slow.

My mind soon filled with more terrible scenes. Before I could even look at the files, Eric Chandler would arrest me—tonight. Or tomorrow I'd face a J.L. who *knew* what I'd done. I'd be alone with him, defenseless.

What would happen to Riley?

Prayers spilled out of me. I couldn't stop them. They'd do no good, I knew. God was done with me. I'd plummeted over a cliff. Made the choice to abandon my soul.

With weary eyes I checked the clock. Fifteen minutes before five. Almost time to pick up Riley. And face my boss's wife and daughter in the process. Riley was sure to be chattering about school. I'd need to match that energy, show my happiness for her— when all I wanted to do was break down and sob. What if they really did come for me tomorrow? Or tonight?

Instead of spending time with my daughter this evening, cherishing our moments together, I'd need to huddle in my room, examining Vince Rayle's documents.

At 5:00 I slipped into my coat and picked up my purse. Locked the office door on the way out. As I dragged my exhausted body to the car, my coat did nothing to keep the chill away. The cold came from inside me.

CHAPTER 24

W hat a house J.L. owned. The exterior was wood and stone, with rough-hewn beams. Even the long driveway through forest was impressive. Quiet hung over the property, the house not visible from the main road.

Rachelle answered the door, all grace and elegance. I stepped inside, into a foyer leading to a huge great room. I could see the kitchen on my left. The house smelled faintly of brownies.

"Thank you for letting Riley stay." Rachelle smiled. "Morgan's enjoying her so much. I'm glad they've found a new friend in each other."

"Me too."

Rachelle pointed. "They're upstairs. Would—"

"Hi, Mom!" Riley appeared at the top of the stairs. "Come see Morgan's room!"

What followed was not only a tour of Morgan's incredibly huge room, but the rest of the upstairs, followed by the entire house. I oohed and aahed at the proper times, impressed with the beauty all around me. But what sticks with me most was the love I saw between Morgan and her mother. How they'd drape an arm around each other's waist, or share a little smile. This was a happy home. One I was willing to tear apart, even now trying to gather evidence against their father and husband.

The small jump drives weighted the purse I had slung over my shoulder. How Morgan and Rachelle would hate me if I did anything to bring J.L. down.

But *he'd* started all this. I had love in my home, too. And if I got in trouble with the law, there was no spouse behind me to take care of *my* daughter.

At the end of the tour we returned to the great room, Riley sliding into her coat. I saw a look pass between her and Morgan.

"Mrs. Westling," Morgan said, "there's—"

"You can call me Cara."

"Okay. Thanks. There's a party Saturday night at another student's house from our school. Will you let Riley come?"

I launched into all the motherly questions you'd expect. What student? How old was he? Where was the party? Who would be there? Rachelle assured me she knew Brandon's parents, and they would be home. She was letting Morgan go without concern. Riley watched the conversation on tenterhooks, her gaze jumping from me to Rachelle. Clearly, my daughter longed to go.

When I agreed, Riley jumped up and down. Morgan tilted her head and raised her eyebrows at Riley, as if to say *see, told you I'd make it happen.*

What a coy expression. Had I just been played by a thirteen-year-old?

Rachelle offered to carpool to the party. I said no. I wanted to take Riley myself, meet Brandon and his parents. Get a feel for their home situation. And I certainly wanted to pick her up, in case the party turned sour.

On the drive home Riley talked nonstop, telling me about the students and teachers at Hayden Prep. Most of all, she talked about her new friends—apparently the girls who hung around with Morgan. I was relieved Riley's first day was a good one. That's all that mattered. She was happy.

But the jump drives in my handbag pulsed.

What could I tell Riley about working on my computer tonight? I couldn't say it was work for J.L. If she happened to mention that to Morgan, and Morgan mentioned it to him …

Riley and I stopped to pick up a pizza, eating it at our kitchen table. Then she wanted to watch TV together, assuring me all her homework was done. I couldn't say no. I needed to be with her. To cherish every moment we had. I have little memory of what we watched. Didn't matter. My thoughts roiled in darkness, hovering over my quaking fear that this would be our last night together. What was Deputy Eric Chandler doing at that moment? Obsessing over every bit of evidence he'd gathered on Paula Tellinger's case? Putting together the facts that would send me to jail?

I *had* to find something on J.L.

At 9:30, when Riley went to her room for the night, I headed straight to my computer. Huddling on my bed, door closed, I inserted the jump drives and copied their contents to my laptop.

Coldness descended on me. I put on a sweater.

First I examined the files from 2011. I ran my eyes down the alphabetized list of names, recognizing them all from the tax preparation packets I'd just labeled.

There. Vince Rayle. A folder, meaning it would contain numerous files. I stared at it, my spine going weak. A little blue icon that could change my entire future. But I didn't even know what to look for. Tax preparation and investment portfolios? I wouldn't spot a problem if I saw it.

I opened the folder and clicked on the top file. Anxiety spat through me, scattering all concentration. I took some deep breaths. Forced myself to focus.

Tax documents came up. I leaned forward, reading the top pages that summarized income and taxes due for Vince's company, Rayle Construction. Total income for that year rounded to $806,000. Total business expenses were virtually the same, leaving no profit to tax.

One thing I had learned already from J.L.—a business owner like Vince Rayle paid himself a salary, which was included in the expenses of the company. The business itself would use every provision possible to lower its taxable income. So to look into Vince's personal taxes I'd need to open the files for him, rather than his company.

But first, was there anything in the company's taxes that looked off?

The return was long, with all kinds of forms attached for various expenses, depreciation, purchases, payments to subcontractors, and on and on. I grabbed a pad of paper and pen, for the next hour noting bottom line totals on the forms. Added up they came to the expense total on the top form.

It all looked right.

Wait a minute.

Well, of course it would. J.L. wouldn't make obvious errors like that. If he was fudging something, it would be hidden in details. And if he was somehow bilking Vince Rayle—giving Paula reason to blackmail him—it wouldn't be in tax returns, right? It would be in investments.

I tipped my head back and gazed at the ceiling. How *stupid*. I'd just wasted an hour on nothing. I should be looking at Vince Rayle's personal tax returns quickly—just to see what he was earning, so I could compare that to any new investments.

No way could I logic through this. I was too tired to think straight.

I threw down the pen. Dragged myself off the bed to stretch. The digital clock on my bedside table read 10:45. At this rate I'd be up all night.

A picture of Riley filled my mind—sleeping in the next room. Innocent and unknowing of any of this. Thinking of nothing but her new school and friends. A life now worth living. A life that could be taken away from her in a heartbeat.

I sat down again on my bed and picked up the laptop. Opened a file titled *Vince Rayle 2011*. I *had* to find something.

That night I worked until I could no longer keep my eyes open. Sometime around 3:00 I finally gave up—after erasing off the jump drives the more current Vince Rayle files copied from my office computer. I'd found no smoking gun. But—something interesting. In 2011 Vince Rayle's personal income was $106,000. The sole source of that income was his construction firm. In 2013 his income had risen to $347,000—over three hundred percent. Again, his salary from the construction company was a little over $100,000. But that year he'd opened a side business—Rayle Trucking. That company's total income was $361,000. According to Vince's personal returns, it had paid him a salary of $245,000.

In 2014 Rayle Trucking made $448,000, paying Vince nearly $300,000. In 2015 and 2016, the numbers rose even higher.

That company was doing mighty well, compared to his construction business.

His investment portfolio from 2013 on reflected his increases in salary. Many more investments. But overall they were doing well. Vince should be happy.

Had Paula somehow discovered the numbers were wrong? Maybe J.L. cooked the books. Maybe he was Payton's version of Bernie Madoff.

But how would Paula know that?

Crawling under the covers, I told myself I'd look at the files again the next night. And on the weekend. If I looked long enough, maybe I'd find something.

I lay in bed exhausted but unable to sleep. Pieces of the puzzle floated in my brain, eluding any interlock. Maybe I was entirely wrong. Maybe Paula's threats to J.L. had nothing to do with Vince. She could have just been out to make some blackmail money on her own—after discovering something else against J.L. Or—this was a crazy idea—what if Vince was in on Paula's scheme? What if they'd both plotted to blackmail J.L. and split the money?

But nothing about Vince Rayle pointed to his being a criminal. He was just a businessman. Although not a very likable one.

That night I got no more than two hours' sleep. As I finally drifted off, one obsession throbbed in my mind. I could plan all I wanted to look at those files again. But if Eric Chandler came for me in the next twelve hours, I would have nothing to prove against J.L.

FRIDAY, NOVEMBER 17

Eric Chandler
Paula Tellinger Disappearance—Questions
6:30 a.m., 11/17

No report of calls from P. since disappearance. ??

Vince Rayle whereabouts Tues. night—STILL CHECKING

~~Cara—J.L. new assistant—nervous. Past run-in with law? CHECK.~~ Record clean.

Search dogs—scent of Paula leading away from area where her car was found. Nothing.

CHAPTER 25

F riday morning I rose like a zombie, enervation and dread in
my chest. The third night in a row with little sleep. Another
day to claw through.

Would I sleep in my own bed tonight? Or in a jail cell?

I had to get those jump drives back in J.L.'s cabinet.

As I blow-dried my hair, a stark realization struck. If I was
arrested that day, they would search my house—and find stolen
documents from J.L.'s office on my computer. More evidence that
I was the criminal. No one would ever believe me.

I threw down the blow dryer and ran to my bedroom. Flung
my computer open and deleted every file I'd so carefully copied the
previous night. Then emptied my computer's trash.

Sweat slicked over my limbs. I paced my room, mind
screaming. Why had I ever copied those files? Couldn't they find
even documents I'd completely deleted?

And now I had no chance to examine them again.

I was done. Beyond help. I collapsed on my bed and cried.

Somehow I pulled myself together to drive Riley to school. We needed to pick up Morgan. Riley noticed my quiet agitation.

"Mom, what's wrong?"

My heart splintered. If she only knew what I had done to our lives.

"I'm ... just tired." I offered her a crooked smile. "Didn't sleep well last night."

Riley gazed at me. "I'm sorry. Is your work hard?"

A tight laugh escaped me. "A little."

Once Morgan joined us, the two girls chatted away about their upcoming party. I drove in silence, jittered by the presence of J.L.'s daughter.

I arrived at work, the jump drives shrieking inside my purse. I set about making the morning coffee.

J.L. wandered out of his office to stand in front of my desk—one foot from where my purse lay on the floor.

"How was Riley's first day at school?"

"Great." My pulse tremored. "She loves the school, and she's met new friends. Morgan has been wonderful. I can't thank you and her enough."

"I'm so glad." J.L. looked pleased with himself. "See? Everything's working."

I forced a smile.

As he walked back to his desk, carrying his coffee mug, I checked his schedule for the day, praying for something that would take him out of the building.

Only in-office appointments.

At 9:00 the first appointment arrived. Sam Merilen. He was tall and wiry, probably in his early sixties. His blue eyes pierced as he greeted me.

"Well, hello there, young lady." He extended his hand. "J.L.'s new sidekick, I see. Glad to see you here."

"Just make sure you only see him here." J.L. raised his eyebrows.

I frowned.

He chuckled. "Sam's the best defense attorney around. Not someone you ever want to need."

Funny, J.L. Real funny.

The two men disappeared into his office.

I pressed my foot against my purse beneath the desk, just to assure myself it was still there.

J.L.'s meeting with Sam Merilen lasted an hour. I tried to concentrate on my work. But my thoughts kept crawling back to Deputy Chandler. What was he doing right now? What new evidence had he gathered?

After the attorney left, fate handed me a gift. J.L. announced he needed to run some errands.

I managed a nod. "Okay."

The door closed like a warning shot behind him.

For a frozen beat I stayed in my chair, hands clenched. What if this was a set-up? What if he knew I had those jump drives?

Like a creeping intruder I sidled toward the window and pressed myself against the wall. Craned my neck to peer out at the street. J.L. was getting into his car.

Heart thumping, I watched him drive away.

I sprang to my desk. My fingers floundered inside my purse, yanking out the jump drives. I ran into J.L.'s office, lunged down to open the cabinet door. Breath on hold, I pulled out the box and laid the jump drives inside, just as I'd found them. Replaced the box on the shelf—

The front office door clicked open.

I stilled, my mind flashing white.

Move, Cara!

My fingers closed the cabinet. I flung myself up straight and jumped to J.L.'s desk. Snatched up his dirty coffee mug.

The door shut.

I gulped in air, forcing calm into my limbs.

Slack-faced, I exited the office.

But it wasn't J.L. Deputy Eric Chandler stood by my desk.

My heart stopped.

I slowed outside my boss's door. "Oh." Did my voice sound tinny? "Hello." I raised the coffee cup. "Just cleaning up after J.L. He's out right now. Running errands."

Eric shifted on his feet. "That's all right. Actually I came to talk to you."

My head detached and floated somewhere above my body.

"Me?" I made it to my desk. Set down the cup. "What can I do for you?"

I leaned against my desk for support. My thoughts fled to Riley. I pictured her in class, called out by the principal. Hearing the shattering news of her mother's arrest.

My knees gave way. I collapsed into my chair.

"Are you okay?" Eric stepped toward me.

I swallowed. "Sorry. Just … tired. My daughter's having issues, and I … didn't sleep well last night."

"Ah." He inclined his chin. "Got it. Been there with my son."

Trenton, wasn't that his name? The boy J.L. had hired at age ten to wash windows. The boy who surely looked to J.L. Larrett as a second father.

I had no chance of being believed here. None.

Eric gave me a smile that quickly faded. "I wanted to ask you a question. I have to admit, I saw J.L. driving off in his car. Thought it would be a good time to catch you."

More questions? Why was he dragging this out? I dropped my hands into my lap, where Eric couldn't see them trembling. "Okay." Should I try to lie my way out of this again? Or spill everything?

"I was wondering if you'd like to have dinner with me tomorrow night."

What?

I gaped at him, seconds ticking by. The words finally sank in, relief drenching me. A laugh tumbled from my mouth.

Eric drew back.

I shook my head. "Oh, I'm sorry. I'm not laughing at your question. I'm just ... so happy it's not about Riley. My daughter. She was bullied at her first school, you see, and we reported it to the principal, and I was ..."

The words ran out, my mouth hanging open. I had to look like an idiot.

"Please, Eric. I am sorry. Forgive me."

He raised a shoulder. "Don't even think about it. I understand."

We looked at each other.

Had J.L. urged Eric to do this? Had he purposely left the office—and let Eric know—so I'd be left here alone?

What could I say to this man? As if I wanted to go out with the deputy who'd arrest me if he knew the truth.

"I ... I really appreciate your invitation, Eric. And I'd like to. The thing is, I—"

Eric's cell phone rang. He let out a frustrated sigh and pulled it from his pocket. Glanced at the caller ID and shot me an apologetic look. "Sorry. I need to take this."

Life is full of irony. In the last minute I'd gone from utter fear to freedom. In the next I would plummet once more. Because the caller's words seeped through Eric's phone, loud enough for me to hear. And my world blew apart.

Eric listened, his expression flickering. "I'll be right there." He slipped the cell back into his pocket, suddenly all business. "Sorry, Cara, I need to respond to this. I'll get back to you, okay?"

My nerves thrummed. "What's happened?"

"Sorry, I can't ... I have to go." He strode to the door and disappeared.

I stared after him, the sentence I'd overheard clanging in my head.

"A hunter found a body in Coeur d'Alene National Forest."

CHAPTER 26

After lunch Riley stood at her locker, pulling out the textbook for her next class. Up and down the hall metal doors banged, students talking and calling to one another. The smell of the cafeteria's meatloaf hung in the air.

Claire appeared beside Riley.

"Hi." She opened her locker.

"Hi."

Awkward silence followed. Riley still felt bad for not standing up for Claire yesterday. "You going to Brandon's party tomorrow?"

Claire stilled, one hand inside her locker. Then she yanked out a book, like she was trying to cover her reaction. "I wasn't invited."

"Oh." Fresh guilt rolled through Riley. "I'm sorry."

Claire shrugged. "Doesn't matter."

Riley knew it did. It mattered a lot. "Could you ask?"

Claire closed her locker and turned to face Riley. "I don't think Morgan wants me there."

"It's not Morgan's party."

"Oh, but it is. Everything is Morgan's around here, haven't you figured that out yet?" Claire gave Riley a knowing smile, like she knew Riley *had*.

"Do you know Morgan almost died four years ago?" Claire hugged her textbook to her chest.

Riley shook her head.

"She had meningitis. Was out of school for a long time."

"Wow. She seems fine now."

"She is." Claire looked around, as if making sure no one could hear. "But at the time it was real bad. Your mom works for her dad, right?"

Great. Everyone at school must know that by now. One more thing to make Riley feel lower than Morgan. "Yeah."

Claire nodded. "I think he's doing better now. Making lots of money again, I mean. When Morgan was sick, I heard he wasn't doing so hot."

"Where'd you hear that?"

"My parents were talking about it." Claire shrugged. "They didn't know I was listening. Mr. Larrett invests their money, like he does for a lot of people around here. He had a lot of people investing in gold, and it fell that year. Like fifty percent or something."

Gold fell? What did that mean? Riley shook her head.

"I'm just saying all the people investing in gold lost money, and so did J.L. Plus, Morgan got sick, and he had to pay huge hospital bills. My parents were saying he might even lose his house."

Riley gawked at Claire. Lose that big house? How? Rich people were … rich. They didn't lose houses and cars and things like poor people did. Like Riley and her mom could.

"Well, so … but he's making money now, right? You're not telling me my mom might lose her job?"

"No, I think he's fine now. 'Cause my parents stayed with him. If he was still losing people's money, they wouldn't be letting him invest theirs anymore."

"Oh." Riley raised her chin in a slow nod. Claire was looking at her like she was supposed to say something. "Why are you telling me this?"

Claire gave her a long look. "Only to tell you that no one's invulnerable. People can fall. Someone popular like Morgan can be fine one minute, then get real sick. Almost die. Somebody rich like her parents can suddenly be not so rich."

"Okay." Riley still didn't get this conversation at all. Was this Claire's way of being all sour grapes because Morgan ignored her?

Frustration crossed Claire's face, like she realized her message wasn't sinking in. "Riley, just ..." She tossed her head and started to walk away, then came back. "Just be who you want to be, is all I'm saying. Don't let somebody else push you around because of who you think they are. It might get you in trouble someday."

With that, she headed off toward class. Riley stared after her, stung. *What?* How could ...? Who did Claire think she was, anyway, some psychiatrist? Like Riley couldn't be who she wanted to be.

She started down the hall, glaring darts at Claire's back.

Who cared what the girl said, anyway? Between the two of them, only one was going to the party tomorrow night. And it wasn't *Claire*.

So there, Miss Know-It-All.

CHAPTER 27

I don't know how long I sat at my desk, immobilized, after Eric left. The world had caved in around me.

J.L. I had to warn him.

I snatched up the office receiver, started dialing his cell—

Wait.

A scenario spun through my mind. Both of us arrested. Phone call history swiped up in a search warrant. *"Mrs. Westling, you see this call made to J.L. Larrett's cell, one minute after Deputy Chandler left ..."*

I banged down the phone.

What should I do? What could I *do*?

I jumped up, fueled by raging energy that could not be channeled.

For half an hour I paced that office, waiting for J.L. to return. When he finally appeared, I pounced on him. I knew I looked wild-eyed and crazed. Who cared?

"They found her!" I carved to a stop in the middle of the office, one hand stuck in my hair.

"What?"

"Paula. They. *Found*. Her."

J.L. blinked. "How do you know?"

"Eric Chandler was here. He got a call. I heard it through his phone."

"Why was he here?"

So J.L. hadn't pushed him to ask me out? "He——. What difference does it make? Somebody found a body in the forest." I spread my arms. "A hunter. Don't *you* hunt? Isn't it hunting season? Why didn't you *think* of this?"

"First of all, calm down." J.L. jabbed his finger toward the door. "If somebody walked in right now, they'd hear you."

"Calm *down*? She won't be just missing anymore; they'll know she's *dead*. What if they find fingerprints on her body—can they do that? On her skin? Clothes? *You said they wouldn't find her, J.L.!*"

"Okay, just …" J.L. held up his hands, fingers spread. "First, we don't know it's her."

"Really? Just how many dead bodies do you think there are in that forest?"

"Second, she's been there for two and a half days."

I shook my head—*so?*

"She may not be in great shape. Lot of animals out there."

I swung away, sick to my stomach. Now to save my own skin, I had to hope Paula Tellinger's body had been torn apart and eaten?

"Cara, all we can do is wait. If they've really found her, we'll hear soon. The whole town will hear."

My head lowered, tears pricking my eyes. "They didn't know. They didn't suspect us at all. Now this. It'll change everything. Now they'll be investigating a homicide."

How could I deal with this? I thought it had been bad before. Now we were supposed to just *wait?* Live our lives, like the sky wasn't blistering above our heads?

My insides heaved. I ran for the bathroom and slammed the door.

When I emerged, stomach emptied and legs weak, J.L. had anchored himself by my desk, legs apart and arms crossed. Like some parent pushed too far.

"Listen to me, you *have* to get hold of yourself. Understand? Or we both go down."

My body sagged. "How could anybody find her, J.L.? She fell such a long way."

He shrugged. "There are other ways to the bottom of that drop-off. Just approach it from the other side."

I gawked at him. "But you told me she *wouldn't* be found because of that cliff. As if nobody could get down there."

"I didn't think anyone would be in that area. It's a good three-mile hike from the nearest service road to the base of that cliff. Not like you can drive there."

"But they *did* go there."

"*Okay,* Cara. I hear you. It won't do any good to argue about it now. Just leave this to me, I'll take care of it."

What was he going to do, wave some magic wand and make her corpse disappear? "How?"

"Don't worry. I'll do it." He stuck his tongue beneath his upper lip and glared at me. "Now, can I count on you? Or is your hysteria gonna be a major shout-out to the Sheriff's Office?"

Heat surged through me. "Hysteria? Really? *You* got me into this, J.L. *You* made me do this. You took my *life*, which I was trying to rebuild—" My voice caught. "And you trashed it. When Paula went over that cliff, I went over, too." Tears rolled down my face. I didn't try to stop them. "That's what you did to me. To my soul. Now I'm trapped, and there's no way out. At least you have Rachelle to take care of Morgan. If I go to jail, what happens to my daughter?"

The last word strangled in my throat. I hung my head and cried.

"We are *not* going to jail, Cara. Not as long as you play your part. I'm telling you they won't be looking our direction. Unless you give them reason to."

"How do you know? You're not above the law, J.L."

His eyes shot daggers. "Are you with me or not? You want to protect your daughter or not?"

"Of *course* I do."

"Then stop your crying. Go about your business—and *stop worrying*." He waved a hand toward my desk. "Do you have work to do for me right now? Work I'm paying you for? Get to it."

He strode into his office and banged the door shut.

I stared after him, throat closing. He could afford to stay calm. Because if push came to shove, he'd put the blame on me. Isn't that what he'd threatened as Paula lay dead at his feet? And nothing from that moment to this had changed. J.L. was the man everyone in the county knew and respected. The man everyone trusted. I was the outsider.

The next few hours blurred. I tried to work. I even tried to pray again. But why should God listen? I was begging Him to protect me from my own sin.

Eric Chandler and other deputies had to be scrambling right now. What would Paula's remains tell them?

"J.L.," I begged, "try to find out what's happening from the Sheriff's Office. And *tell* me."

"Get back to work, Cara."

In the afternoon word streamed through town. A body had been found. Multiple clients called, everyone wanting to be the first to inform J.L. Did he think it was Paula? And, of course, Riley phoned my cell. The news had reached school.

"Mom, they found a dead body in the forest! It's probably that Paula!"

My eyes shut. "I heard."

"Somebody *killed* her!"

"You don't know that. We don't even know yet that it's her. Even if it is, maybe she was just hiking and fell. Be careful not to listen to rumors."

"Why would she go hiking after she was at your office? It was getting dark by then, right?"

"Riley, we *don't* know it's her."

"But it probably is. And she was right there just before that, talking to you!"

The conversation was more than I could bear. I had to get off the phone. "Look, I have to go now. We'll talk about this later."

I smacked the *off* button and stared at my hands, appalled at what they'd done to another human being. Surely they belonged to someone else. Not me.

Not me.

The final call came from Vince Rayle. I recognized his voice. He sounded upset. I put him through to J.L., then kept an eye on the red phone button that indicated they were still speaking. When the red light went out, J.L. emerged from his office.

"Stay calm," he said. "And I'll tell you something."

My chest convulsed.

"Paula's roommate went in to look at the body. She's been identified."

Identified.

Which meant she hadn't been torn apart.

We were done. My life was *over.* "What if they find evidence on her?"

For once, J.L had nothing to say.

SATURDAY, NOVEMBER 18

CHAPTER 28

Riley woke up Saturday thinking about that dead woman in the forest. It *was* Paula Tellinger. Riley had gotten texts last night from friends at school, telling her the news.

How creepy that her mom had been with someone who would soon be dead. That's probably why she hadn't wanted to talk about it. It must be creeping her out, too.

Riley pushed the thoughts away. It's not like they knew the woman. Besides, she had better things to think about—like the party that night! She lazed in bed for awhile, her excitement growing, then got up and started sorting through her clothes. What hadn't she worn yet to school? What outfit would make her look so cool that everybody's head would turn when she walked into Brandon's house?

If only she had designer clothes like Morgan.

Riley finally decided on a red top and jeans. Maybe she could fix her hair some, using her mom's curling iron. And she should do her nails. She had blue polish sitting around somewhere.

She and Morgan texted back and forth about the party. Morgan said she was shopping with her mom for a new outfit. Of course.

Her dad was out hunting.

When Riley went into the kitchen for something to eat, she found her mom slumped over a cup of coffee at the table. She had circles under her eyes. Didn't look like she'd slept much.

"What's wrong? Are you thinking about Paula?"

Mom took a deep breath. "No, no. I mean, that is sad, but … I'm just tired." She made a funny little smile.

"Are you sick?"

"No."

"Okay, good. Don't forget you're taking me to the party. It starts at 7:00."

"I haven't forgotten."

Riley's mom kept looking at her. "You're so pretty. Come here." She held out her arms.

Riley went over and bent down for a hug. Mom drew her close and didn't want to let go. "I love you, Riley. I never want to be without you."

What was going on?

"I don't want to be without you, either." Riley's words muffled into her mom's shoulder.

When she pulled away and straightened she saw tears in her mother's eyes. Riley stiffened.

"What's *wrong*? Something's going on."

Mom shook her head. "Nothing. I'm just tired."

"From work?"

"Yeah."

"You sure? This isn't about Paula?"

"Yes, I'm sure. And no, it's not."

Riley knew something *was* wrong. She could feel it. She sat down at the table. "You *sure* everything's okay?" So much had been terrible in their lives. Things were just beginning to turn around ... "Stop worrying. I'm fine."

Riley sat back in her chair. Maybe it *was* just tiredness. Guilt twinged inside her. Mom worked so hard for them both, doing all she could. And here Riley was, not being thankful. Wishing she had better clothes.

Her mind flashed to the conversation with Claire. Rich people could have money troubles, too.

"I heard something about Morgan and her parents yesterday."

"Oh?" Mom took a slow drink of coffee.

"Yeah. She was real sick four years ago. She almost died."

"Yes. Her father told me about that."

"Did he tell you they lost a lot of money?"

Mom shook her head. "What do you mean?"

"They had a lot of hospital bills. Plus, her dad invested in gold, and that ... I don't know, fell or something. Does that make sense? So he and a lot of his clients lost money. They were even afraid of losing their house."

Riley's mom tilted her head. "How do you know this?"

"A girl at school told me. Claire. She heard her parents talking back then. About J.L. and his money and everything. But then after awhile he was okay and making lots of money again."

Her mom's gaze dropped to the table. She frowned. "Well, Riley. That's just gossip, you know."

"I know."

"Morgan wouldn't be too happy if she heard you talking about that to other people."

No kidding. "I'm not telling anybody. Just you."

Mom nodded.

They sat in silence.

"I've been texting with Morgan. She's buying new clothes for the party."

"Oh. I'm so sorry I can't buy you anything."

"That's okay, I didn't mean ..." Great, now she'd just made her mom feel worse. "Her dad's out hunting. Deer, I think. Poor Bambis."

Mom managed a smile. "They don't shoot baby deer, Riley. Just bucks."

"I know."

More silence.

Mom really did look more than just tired. Something was bothering her big time. Riley's nerves tingled. "Did you hear from Dad or something?"

"No. What makes you ask that?"

"Nothing."

Mom sighed. "You're really happy at that school, aren't you."

Oh, no. Riley's heart stalled. "I don't have to stop going, do I? Mr. Larrett's still paying for it?"

"Yes. Don't worry." Her mom tried to smile again. But her mouth went crooked.

Riley couldn't take any more. She pushed back her chair and stood. Whatever this was, whatever was going on with her mom— she didn't want to know. Her life was going too good right now. New school. Friends. A *party.* Nothing could get in the way of all that. Nothing.

Please.

She had to get out of the kitchen.

"I'm gonna go paint my nails." She started toward her bedroom.

"You need to eat breakfast."

"Later. Promise."

Riley hurried out of the room before her mom could say anything else. Something that might ruin her day and bring her world tumbling down, like it had so many times before. That couldn't happen. Not again. Not *now*.

She reached her room and started raking through her drawers for the nail polish.

Nothing was wrong with her mom. For sure. Riley had read too much into her expression. Mom was just tired, like she said. Everything was fine. Just fine.

Riley found the polish. She snatched it from her drawer and channeled all her concentration into painting her nails.

Eric Chandler
Paula Tellinger Homicide—Autopsy follow-up/Notes
10:30 a.m., 11/18

Cause of death: strangulation. Scarf used?

White scarf not on body. Where?

Sweater—red. Roommate Linda said she wore red.
Cara Westling said didn't remember color. Margie
said blue. ??

Nail polish—white. Right forefinger—chip. Match size/
color of chip in car trunk. Paula transported to forest
in trunk? Bring in cadaver dog to examine trunk.

Recheck alibis for persons of interest.

House key found near body. Whose?

CHAPTER 29

Friday night had been my fourth with little sleep. Saturday morning I could barely drag myself into the kitchen. But after I talked to Riley, the strangest feeling came over me. I became possessed by a terror-driven energy. It built up ... built up ... until it raged and churned inside me, and I didn't know how to dispel it. I ended up cleaning house with a fury. I vacuumed, and dusted, and scrubbed the bathroom and kitchen floor. But as I gritted my teeth and shoved a hand brush over the kitchen tile, my mind would not turn off. Had they performed the autopsy? What did they find? How many pieces of evidence would lead to me?

The house is small, and we hadn't lived in it that long. After an hour and a half I was done. What to do with my energy now?

How to survive the rest of the weekend?

Deputy Chandler had never called back on Friday regarding our date. And he wouldn't call now. He'd be working on the homicide case twenty-four/seven. At least I didn't have to deal with saying no to his invitation to dinner.

As I put away the cleaning brush and gloves under the sink, Riley's words echoed. *"Morgan was sick four years ago … they lost a lot of money."*

I closed the cabinet and straightened. Stared at a chipped tile on the counter, thinking.

Four years ago. The year 2013. That was the year Vince Rayle started the new company that was making him so much money— Rayle Trucking.

I folded my arms and leaned against the counter. So what? Probably coincidence. Or maybe it was just fortunate on J.L.'s part. When his business was down and he had mounting personal bills, one of his clients started making a lot of money. The additional successful investments he made for that client earned J.L. more income and pulled him out of his medical debts.

"After awhile he was okay and making lots of money again."

How long after?

A dank shadow descended over me.

When I'd looked at Vince Rayle's files, I hadn't examined all the individual expense forms attached to Rayle Trucking. What exactly did that company do?

But how to find out now? I'd erased all the documents from my computer.

I wandered into the living room and sank down on the couch. Maybe this was nothing. Just grasping at straws.

Still, it was the only straw I had.

I pushed to my feet and went to my room. Opened my computer and sat cross-legged on my bed, searching *Rayle Trucking Payton Idaho* online. The company must at least have a website.

I found none. In fact, I saw nothing about the company.

But it did exist. I'd seen the tax returns.

Did the business transport goods, as its name implied? Whose? Without any marketing, how did they find their clients?

I closed the computer and slid off the bed. Thrust a hand in my hair, trying to think.

The files I needed were at the office.

And J.L. was out hunting.

At least that's what he'd told his family.

Such a risk, going to the office on a Saturday. What reason could I possibly give J.L. if he walked in the door? And if in the future he noticed I'd accessed files on the weekend—what then?

Fragmented scenes of the choice gone bad jagged through my head.

But if I did not go, how to fight back? I'd rattle around the house for the next two days, waiting for the sky to cave.

My feet took me into Riley's bedroom. "Hey." I pinned on a smile. "Think you'd be all right here for an hour or so if I went to the office and caught up on some work?"

"Sure."

Such a nonchalant answer. "Great." I started to turn away, then hesitated. "Probably best if you don't mention this to Morgan, okay? I don't want her dad to think I'm behind."

Riley shrugged. "Okay."

Soon I was backing out of the garage. I drove to the office, my gaze flicking over the streets, watching for J.L.'s car. No sign of him. And his SUV was not parked outside our office building.

My muscles turned to granite as I unlocked the entrance to Larrett Financial.

Once inside I locked the door. The metallic sound of J.L.'s inserted key would at least give me a few seconds to close files on my computer.

I hurried to the cabinet in J.L.'s office and took out the jump drives that contained the 2013 through 2015 files on Rayle Trucking. The more recent years sat on my computer.

At my desk I thrust back my shoulders, raking in air. What was I *doing?* If J.L. showed up ...

My hands fumbled as I pushed in a jump drive.

Perched forward in my chair, I opened the 2013 file on Rayle Trucking. Scrolled through every form. What to look for? My mind could only half focus, my head cocked for any sound from outside the door. Then something caught my attention. Rayle Trucking must transport a lot of goods to make so much money, right? So why did the equipment depreciation form show only four trucks? In other forms I saw records for mileage to and from Canada.

What were the trucks taking there?

My mouth dried out. I would not stop to get a glass of water.

I scanned the 2014 through 2016 files but couldn't decipher anything new. Whatever the company was into, it was doing more of it—and making more money.

Unanswered questions needled me.

An hour stumbled by. My neck and back cramped. Still, I could find nothing more. Paula Tellinger was dead. But apparently Rayle Trucking was not the reason why.

And I'd dared to think I could be some valiant warrior who triumphed over J.L. Larrett.

Where was Eric Chandler right now? On his way to my house, arrest warrant in hand?

Oh, Riley. I had failed her so badly.

Blurry-eyed, I replaced the jump drives in their cabinet. Grabbed my purse and turned toward the door—

Wait.

I stared at my computer.

Quickly I switched it back on. Looked up the cell number for J.L.'s client, Sam Merilen, "the best defense attorney around," and wrote it down.

Stone-faced, dead inside, I slipped out of J.L.'s office and went home to spend whatever remaining freedom I had with my daughter.

CHAPTER 30

Riley's heart fluttered on the way to Brandon's house. If only her mom hadn't insisted on taking her to the party. She'd much rather have gone with Morgan. This way Riley could end up arriving alone if Morgan and her friends weren't there yet. Riley had done her best to make sure that didn't happen, texting all of them to see when they'd get there. And she'd hung back from leaving home until at least Alissa and Bella were on their way. But what if they made a last-minute stop or something?

Riley's mom had trouble finding Brandon's address, even using her phone's GPS. She seemed like her mind was so far away. And Riley still didn't want to ask why—for fear of the answer. Brandon lived on Hayden Lake, and some of the roads were narrow. Plus, it was dark. Finally, they pulled up to a pretty house with a big porch and all the lights on.

Sweat popped out on Riley's forehead. She couldn't open her door.

Mom turned toward her. "You okay?"

"Yeah."

Mom nodded. "You're going to be fine, you know. You've been fine at school, and most of these kids are from there, right?"

"Yeah." Riley's throat turned to cotton. What if everything good that had happened at school fell apart tonight? What if suddenly some person didn't like her, and they all started talking about her?

But Morgan wouldn't allow that.

What if that person turned out to be *Morgan?*

Riley looked out her window so Mom couldn't see her face. She did *not* want to cry. Life could be so overwhelming. And her emotions were up and down. It got really tiring dealing with happiness one minute and fear the next.

Mom laid a hand on Riley's arm. "If anything goes wrong, call me. I'll come get you right away."

Sure, but that would take fifteen minutes. A lot could happen in that amount of time. Not to mention, Riley would have to face everyone at school on Monday.

Her mom leaned back against the seat. "It's okay. We can sit here until you're ready."

Riley nodded. She closed her eyes for a minute and asked God to *please, please help*. Then she took a deep breath—and forced herself to open the car door. If she didn't do it right then, she may not do it at all.

Mom walked Riley to Brandon's front door so she could meet his parents. Riley had thought that would be embarrassing, but right now she was glad for the company.

Brandon's mom answered the door. "Come in, come in." She was tall and looked a lot older than Riley's mother. As soon as they stepped inside, Riley could hear music coming from downstairs. Fresh panic washed over her.

"You're the new girl." Brandon's mom smiled at Riley after introductions. Her name was Sharon. "So glad you could come."

The new girl. Riley managed a nod.

The adults talked for awhile, Brandon's mom saying that she and her husband—who was upstairs at the moment—would be "checking on the kids regularly." Riley cringed at the questions her mom asked. At least none of her friends could hear. They'd think her mom totally ran her life.

"Go on downstairs if you like, Riley." Brandon's mom pointed. "Through that door right there. Morgan asked me to tell you she's already here."

She *was?* Relief flooded Riley. "Okay. 'Bye, Mom." She headed for the stairs.

When she opened the door, the music got louder.

"Hey!" Morgan called as soon as Riley hit the last stair. "Over here!"

The basement was one huge room with a couple of closed doors on either side. In the middle of the room stood a table holding all kinds of snacks and drinks. At the far end of the room a sliding door led out to a covered deck. A light was on out there, illuminating part of the backyard. Beyond it, the lake shimmered under a half moon. So pretty.

Wow, would Riley love to have a house like this. She'd spend all day staring out at the lake. And swimming in it during summer.

Morgan was surrounded by Alissa, Bella, Brandon, Taryn, and a bunch of other students—maybe twenty altogether. An equal number of guys and girls. Riley had met most of them. She could only remember some of their names. Ryan, Tommy, Chester, Meg, Holly. A lot of them were in Brandon's ninth grade class. Everyone was talking and laughing and kidding each other. And eating junk food. Brandon had his arm around Taryn's shoulder. He looked like a football player, and Taryn stood a good foot shorter. With her tiny waist and hips, she had to be a size zero.

Grant, the guy Riley liked at school, hadn't been invited. If only he was there.

Morgan took her arm and pulled her closer in. "Come on, help me eat all this popcorn. Open your mouth."

Soon Morgan was throwing popcorn for Riley to catch in her mouth. Turned out she was good at it, and Morgan moved farther and farther away. The more Riley caught, the more everyone cheered.

By the time they tired of the game, Riley felt like she belonged.

Lauren showed up, talking a blue streak as usual, and the noise in the room rose. "Oh, you would not *believe* my dad." Lauren struck a pose and laid the back of her hand against her forehead.

Morgan whispered in Riley's ear. "Her dad's twenty years older than her mom."

Riley raised her chin in a nod.

"I told him"—Lauren was now waving her hand in the air— "Justin Bieber was gonna be here tonight."

"Whoa!" Alissa did a dance step, and everyone laughed.

"And he says, 'Who's Justin Bieber?'"

The girls howled at that. And some guy Riley didn't know said, "Yeah, who is that?"

Morgan pushed him. "Aw, you're just jealous."

And on like that it went. Riley found herself joining in, making jokes. Her cheeks felt warm with excitement, and it was all she could do not to dance around like Alissa. She *belonged.* This was *her group* now. She didn't have to be scared anymore.

All because of Morgan. And her dad, who'd paid for Riley's tuition in the first place.

Riley had to do something especially nice for them. What, she didn't know. What could she possibly give *them?*

Every once in awhile Brandon's mom would come downstairs. She'd check the food and drinks, bringing more when needed. But it was clear she was also checking on everybody there.

Time went by so fast. When Morgan answered a call on her cell, Riley pulled out her own phone. Eight-thirty. The party was already half over. Her mom was coming to get her at 10:00.

Morgan clicked off her call and motioned Riley away from the crowd. "I have to go to the bathroom," she said in Riley's ear. "Remember I told you about Blaze, my boyfriend? I've been watching for him. If he shows up while I'm gone, would you let him in?" She pointed toward the sliding glass door. "'Cause, remember, you're the only one who knows about him. You'll have to keep watch and let him in real fast."

Riley nodded, glad to help. "Sure."

Morgan smiled. "Thanks." She disappeared into the bathroom.

Riley wandered over to the food table, her eye on the glass door. If Blaze showed up, she was ready. Anything for Morgan.

Within a minute—he appeared outside. Just like that.

Riley swiveled her head right and left. No one else noticed him. They were all huddled in a loud circle, playing another game. She hurried to the door, unlocked the bolt, and slid it back.

Blaze brushed past her as he entered. "Thanks." He was tall and dark-haired, and his voice sounded deep. Behind him trailed the smell of alcohol. His eyes scanned the room, looking for Morgan.

"She'll be out in a minute." Riley slid the door closed and locked it.

Alissa happened to look up from the circle, spotting Blaze. She looked from him to Riley. "Hi." Surprise laced her voice. Others turned to see.

Riley's cheeks went hot. She felt spotlighted, standing next to some older guy who hadn't been invited.

Morgan stepped out of the bathroom. "Oh, hi!" she called to Blaze.

"Hey."

He just stood there, one hand at his side, the other scratching his waist. Not making any move toward Morgan. A weird vibe came off him. Riley stepped away.

By now everyone was gawking at him.

"Everybody." Morgan walked toward him. "Meet Blaze. Riley just let him in. I heard he might be stopping by."

Wait—"Riley let him in?" As if he was *her* friend?

Morgan approached Blaze and took his arm. "Brandon, you don't mind, do you? He'll just stay a little while. We should make him feel welcome."

Brandon waved a hand. "No problem."

Alissa, Lauren, and Bella gazed back and forth between Blaze and Riley, as if amazed the "new girl" had the nerve to invite some outsider to the party.

"Thanks." Morgan pulled Blaze forward. "Come sit on the couch with me."

Riley stayed near the door. What was she supposed to do now?

Most of the others turned back to their game. Alissa, Bella, and Lauren wandered over to the couch to meet Blaze. Riley sidled over as well. She could still feel their eyes on her, judging. Until Blaze draped his arm around Morgan and pulled her close. Clearly those two had some kind of history, and Morgan wasn't trying to hide it. Riley was just caught in the middle. The three girls' expressions flattened. They exchanged glances, silently sharing their understanding, then looked again at Riley. She had the same distinct feeling as in class two days ago when Morgan had been so dismissive of Grant just because he didn't pay her enough attention. As if Morgan pulled the strings around here, and no one dared speak against her. As if, like all of them at one time or another, Riley had just been seriously *used*.

This had all been a set-up.

"Don't let somebody else push you around because of who you think they are," Claire had said. *"It might get you in trouble someday."*

Was this the reason Morgan had told no one else about Blaze? Had she planned this, even as she and Riley sat on her bed two days ago?

Brandon came over to the couch, gazing down at Blaze. "Listen, my mom's gonna get all upset if she sees you here. She could come down anytime."

"Yeah, I know." Morgan stood, holding out her hand to Blaze. "He can just go in there for awhile." She pointed to a bedroom. "Out of sight."

Brandon gave her a long look, as if seeing right through her. "Don't be doing anything that'll get me in trouble. Or we won't be having any more parties here."

Morgan laughed. "You worry too much."

Alissa, Lauren, and Bella shuffled backward, giving Morgan space to walk away arm-in-arm with Blaze. Riley moved back, too, suddenly feeling more aligned with the three girls than Morgan. Soon they and Brandon were rejoining the noisy game. But Riley turned to watch Morgan and Blaze enter the bedroom. What were they going to do in there?

Whatever it was, if they were caught, no way Riley could be blamed for it.

She shivered. Something about Blaze made her skin crawl. He seemed ... off. His movements were slow, almost sleepy. And when she'd looked into his eyes, his pupils were so tiny. Was he high on something? Drunk?

This is the kind of guy Morgan liked?

Riley turned back toward the others. She tried to join in, but without Morgan right there, she didn't feel as safe. Which was a problem, because how safe would she now feel being *near* Morgan? She glanced toward the bedroom. The door was closed.

It wasn't long after that—maybe ten minutes—when everything fell apart.

Riley was at the food table, filling a small bowl with popcorn, when the bedroom door flew open. Morgan stumbled out, her hair messy and panic on her face.

"Help! Something's wrong with him!"

Brandon and Taryn were sitting on the couch where Blaze had been. Brandon jumped up. "What?"

"*Help him!*"

Brandon ran into the bedroom, followed by Taryn. Everyone else tried to crowd in. Riley hung back, shudders running down her spine. Hadn't she known something was wrong with Blaze?

Voices shouted from the bedroom. Morgan sobbed. Riley couldn't see what was going on.

"Get back, let him breathe!" Brandon's voice.

"It's too hot in here, pull him out of the room!" Ryan said.

More commotion, lots of shuffling and grunting. Girls spilled out of the bedroom, Alissa with her arm around a crying Morgan. Brandon came out next, his hands under Blaze's armpits. Ryan had his feet. Blaze's eyes were closed.

They carried him to the middle of the room and laid him on the floor. Riley and everyone else circled around, gawking. Blaze's head sagged to one side. His skin was pasty, and his breathing sounded funny.

Brandon fell to his knees beside him. "What happened?"

"I d-don't *know!*" Morgan could hardly speak.

"Did he take something?"

"No! We were just sitting on the bed. He looked so tired. Then he laid down and went to sleep. I couldn't wake him up!"

"Blaze!" Brandon smacked both of his cheeks. "Hey, man!"

Blaze's head bounced around like a puppet's. Brandon hit him again.

"Wait, listen." Ryan leaned down. "Is he breathing?"

"Everybody be quiet." Brandon laid his head on Blaze's chest. Then straightened. "Barely. We have to call 911."

"No!" Morgan waved her hands. "He's not supposed to be here; can't we just help him?"

"How?" Brandon looked up at her. "I think he's on something."

"I'm telling you he didn't take *anything.*"

"He could have done it before he came." Brandon swiveled his head toward Riley. "Do you know?"

Everyone's eyes turned on her. Riley's cheeks flamed. Why should *she* know? She shook her head.

"He *has* to wake up!" Morgan threw herself down next to Blaze. "Come on, Blaze, come on!" She shook him like a rag doll, panic spilling out of her mouth. "You can't—"

Brandon jumped up and pulled her off. "Stop! It's not working."

Morgan stumbled back, wracked with sobs. Bella and Lauren hugged her. Terror swept through the room. What were they going to *do?* A guy was dying right in front of them.

Brandon snatched his phone from his pocket.

Morgan's face contorted. "No! You can't call!"

"Why?"

"Because ... because Riley will get in trouble."

Riley's eyes bugged. For the second time everybody focused on her.

Morgan swiped at her cheeks. "She's the one who let him in here."

Riley's mouth opened, but nothing came out.

Brandon threw Morgan a hard look, then jerked his chin toward Taryn. "Go get my parents."

Taryn ran for the stairs.

Brandon held up his phone and smacked in 911.

Eric Chandler
Paula Tellinger Homicide—Notes to follow up
8:30 p.m., 11/18

Tip re: dumpster. Check.

Paula's purse/cell phone still missing. Where?

House key found near body—still unidentified.

CHAPTER 31

I slumped on my couch, staring mindlessly at the television, when headlights washed over the front of my house.

Immediately—I knew.

Leaning sideways, I peered out the window. A deputy's car sat in my driveway.

My mind turned to deadwood.

Somehow, I pushed to my feet.

Through the sheer curtains I watched as Eric Chandler got out and walked the short distance to the porch. I knew he could see me. My legs had gone to stone.

The doorbell rang.

I stared toward the sound, reality flipping in slow motion through my brain. Just a few inches' thickness of wood stood between my freedom—and the beginning of the rest of my life.

As I opened the door my heart struggled to beat.

Eric Chandler nodded at me. "Cara. Sorry to bother you this evening."

"That's okay." Automatic words.

He shifted his feet. "Look, I wish I was here picking you up for dinner. Instead—you know I'm working this case. I need to ask you to come down to headquarters with me for some additional questioning."

How surreal. A would-be date turning into an arrest. "Questions about what? I've told you everything I know."

"I'll talk to you about it when we get there."

"Can't we do it here?"

"We'd rather you come to us. Just easier that way."

Come to us. Sure. In an interrogation room with cameras. So they could tape my every word and expression.

"Actually." I checked my watch. "I can't do that right now. I have to pick up my daughter at a party in Hayden at 10:00."

"Can someone else do that for you?"

"No."

We stared at each other. I placed a hand on the door threshold to steady myself.

"All right. Perhaps you can come in tomorrow morning."

My stare went blank. He wasn't going to arrest me now?

That could only mean one thing. They didn't have all the evidence they needed yet. Eric would work to pry a confession from me. If I talked to him tomorrow, I could not go without a lawyer. But wouldn't taking an attorney just make me look more guilty?

I'd just refuse to go.

Could they make me?

"Sure. I'll … I'll look into it tomorrow, okay?"

"Good. What time will you be there?"

"Do I have to figure this out right now?"

"It would be helpful, yes."

"Okay, eleven o'clock." I just wanted the man off my porch.

"Eleven it is. We're in Coeur d'Alene, you know."

"I'll find it."

"Thanks." Eric turned to go. "Sorry again to bother you."

Such politeness. For the time being. Imagine how quickly that would change once he had me pinned like an insect in some little room.

As I stepped back, I heard his portable radio go off. I closed the door before I could make out any words from the call. It could have been for anything. Domestic violence, a robbery. But later I would wonder—by some timely (or untimely) coincidence, could it have been about a possible drug overdose at a party in Hayden?

I sank against the door, trying to breathe. That's when my cell phone sounded. Riley's ringtone.

Only 9:15. Something had gone wrong.

I tapped on the call. "Riley, you okay?"

She burst into tears.

Oh, no. "What is it?"

She could only cry. I sank down on the couch and closed my eyes. Tried to prepare myself for whatever I was about to hear.

"He—I think he might *die!*" My daughter sobbed.

"What? Who?"

"B-Blaze. This guy at the party. We called 911, and the paramedics are here, and I don't even know if he's *breathing* anymore!" The last word rose in a wail.

"Why, what happened to him?"

"I don't *know.* Brandon said he thought he took drugs. But all I know is it's gonna be all my fault, and everybody's gonna blame *me.*"

Drugs?

"What do you mean, why should they blame you?"

"Because I let him *in*!"

None of this was making sense. I struggled back to my feet. "I'm coming to get you right now. Be there in fifteen minutes. Call me if you need to, I'll be in the car."

No answer. Just more crying.

"Riley, hear me?" I snatched up my purse and coat.

"Y-yes."

"Okay. Hang in there. See you soon."

I ended the call and ran out the door.

CHAPTER 32

C ars littered the street outside Brandon's house. Parents had descended to rescue their kids from the disastrous party. No ambulance in sight. I drove some distance down the lane before spotting a place to pull over.

Riley had not called me back.

I ran down the road and up the porch steps. Colliding voices—adult and teenaged—filtered through the door. I pushed it open.

A dozen or so parents and their kids, most of whom I didn't know, crowded the living room. Rachelle stood at the far end, holding Morgan. She was crying. Brandon's dad peppered him with questions, other grim-faced parents looking on.

Where was Riley?

"Cara, right?" Brandon's mother, Sharon, appeared at my side, her forehead creased and cheeks pale. "I'm so sorry. Nothing like this has ever—"

"What happened?"

The story spilled out. Some older boy, not invited, showed up at the house. He collapsed. Paramedics took him away. Suspected drug overdose.

Drugs. *Here.* At a party I'd been assured was *safe.*

Sharon couldn't miss the expression on my face. She laced her hands, pressing them to her chest. "He got in through the basement door—we never saw him. I'm so sorry. None of the kids saw him taking drugs, I can assure you of that. He took them before he got here."

A teenager, collapsed from drugs. Imagine the pain of his parents. "How is he?"

Sharon shook her head. "We don't know. He was unresponsive when they left."

Unresponsive. This poor boy could die?

I brushed hair away from my face. "Will someone from the hospital let you know how he's doing?"

Sharon hesitated. "I don't … our kids don't know him. He's not from Hayden Prep."

Our kids?

The judging gaze of every person in the room settled on me.

Brandon's father spoke up. "We thought Riley knew him."

"Why would you think that? She's new in town, she hardly knows anyone."

At that moment Morgan's eyes met mine. She looked away.

What was going on?

"Riley's the one who let him into the house." Sharon's voice edged with accusation.

The silence in the room stung. "What do you *mean*, she let him in?"

"Ask your daughter. That's what the other kids told me. There's a back door in the basement. She was near that door when he showed up. She let him right in. Like she'd been waiting for him."

"Everybody's gonna blame me!"

I cast a searing glance around the room. If I was feeling their stares of blame, what must Riley have been through?

"*Where* is she?"

"Downstairs."

In the basement, by herself. While everyone else stood up here and talked about her.

I spun on my heel toward the door at the top of the stairs. Strode through and smacked it shut behind me.

The smell hit as I descended. The odor of teenage sweat and terror. Of recent chaos.

"Riley?" I clattered down the steps. "Riley?"

She slouched on the sofa, knees drawn up to her chest, hugging her legs. That picture of her, all alone and crying—even now it pierces my heart. What had she done that turned her into a pariah in such a short time?

"Riley." I ran to her and sank down on the couch. She leaned against me and sobbed.

I held her, rubbing her shoulder. How had I failed—again—to protect my daughter? Why had she been handed such a difficult life?

After some time, she drew away, wiping her nose. I pulled tissues from my purse and pressed them into her hand. "It's going to be okay. Just tell me what happened."

And she did. With her head hung and voice wobbling, she started with the beginning of the party, when all felt wonderful and fun, to the moment the paramedics carried the boy called Blaze out the door on a gurney. "It was so *awful*. He was blue, and his breathing was all funny. I thought he was going to die right in front of us. Everyone did. And he still might. When they carried him out, he *looked* like he was dead."

"I'm so sorry." I stroked her cheek. "The doctors will do everything they can for him."

Riley blinked tears onto her lap.

"So what happened after he was gone?"

Brandon's mother and father had demanded answers, that's what. And the other kids swung into self-defense.

"Why'd you let him in here, Riley?" Redness had mottled Brandon's neck.

"I—" Riley wanted to melt into the floor. Couldn't everybody see that Blaze was Morgan's friend, not hers? Morgan had been in the *bedroom* with him. Alissa, Lauren, and Bella—they knew what had happened. But they just stared at her. Riley cast a helpless look at Morgan, but she wasn't about to help.

"What if he *dies?*" Morgan fell to her knees and cried. Brandon's mom rushed over to comfort her. And then it was all about wonderful Morgan and her compassion for a boy she didn't even know, almost as if Riley had forced drugs down Blaze's throat.

What could Riley say at that point? Everyone else was protecting Princess Morgan. Riley knew if she told what really happened, they'd all deny it. Call her a liar and never be her friends again.

When Riley finished telling me her story, she sank back against the couch, exhausted. "They won't like me now, anyway. They'll have to keep pretending this was my fault, to keep themselves out of trouble." She sniffed.

I pulled her close again.

"What's wrong with me, Mom?" The words muffled into my shoulder. "Everywhere I go it's the same thing. It's *me*. I'm just ... bad."

"No, Riley, you are *not*."

I wanted to hit something, put my fist through the wall. To hear my daughter talk about herself like that! This was all thanks to Morgan. A girl who, just like her father, believed she could control everyone around her. Mr. and Miss Entitled.

I should have known she was too friendly to be true.

"Don't you ever say that about yourself, Riley. Sometimes life does bad things to innocent people. Other people put them in terrible situations. The world's not always a good place, and choices others make—we can get caught in the fallout. Somehow in the midst of it, we have to stay strong. Keep doing what's right."

Her breath shuddered. "How did you do it? With Dad, and the way he treated you and everything?"

"I prayed a lot. Couldn't have done it without God's help."

But I'd cut that prayer lifeline now, hadn't I? Through my own wrong actions.

I nudged Riley. "Let's go home. And I'm not just going to let this be, you understand. I'm telling Brandon's parents and Rachelle what really happened."

Riley jerked up straight, her face pinched. "No! You can't. They'll hate me."

"It's the truth, Riley. You want to be a slave to their lie? To what Morgan did?"

Riley turned away. She looked so young. Frightened. "I can't keep changing schools." Her voice was barely audible.

My eyes slipped shut. She was right. I could protect her here, tonight, make sure everyone heard the real story. But I couldn't go to school with her. Couldn't live her life.

All I could do was be her role model. Walk in strength and truth.

And how's that working for you, Mom of the Year?

I heaved a sigh. "Come on. Let's get out of here."

We struggled to our feet.

"Promise me you won't say anything, Mom." Riley was shaking. "*Please.*"

"Riley, I am so mad right now, I can't promise you anything. Except that I love you."

We dragged ourselves up the stairs. When we reached the main level, Morgan and Rachelle were already gone. Just as well. I don't know what I might have said to that girl. Many of the other kids had also left. Three still needed to be picked up. Brandon and his parents stood in their living room, as if waiting for the guilty party to reappear.

My hand clamped protectively onto Riley's arm. She would not raise her eyes from the floor.

Facing Brandon's mother, I planed my voice into steadiness. "I suggest you talk to your son about what really happened."

"What do you mean?"

I turned a narrow-eyed gaze on Brandon. "Aren't you a year older than Morgan?"

He nodded.

"You going to let her dictate what you do and say? You going to let her hide behind her lie?"

I stared him down until he glanced away.

"You're growing up, Brandon. Be a man about this."

His mother thrust back her shoulders. "Now wait a—"

I jerked my hand up, palm out. "Just talk to him. I'm sure he'll do the right thing." I looked from her to Brandon's father.

"I'm taking my daughter home now. She's been through enough accusation for one night."

Riley and I let ourselves out, stepping onto the porch and into the cold night air. Somehow I managed to close the front door without slamming it.

SUNDAY, NOVEMBER 19

CHAPTER 33

S aturday night—the fifth since my nightmare began. And
once again, little sleep.

My thoughts twisted from Riley ... to prison ... to J.L. ...
to Morgan ... and back again. My tears were all for Riley. As if
she wasn't already going through enough. Imagine what her life
would be like when I was arrested. Placed in the system, farmed
out to some foster home. Pointed at and talked about as the
daughter of a murderer. And she'd be forced back to public school
with those horrible bullies. J.L. would hardly keep paying for her
tuition at Hayden Prep after I "claimed" he killed Paula. The town
would rally around J.L. Larrett, their hero, and Morgan, his sweet
daughter who'd tried to befriend mine. Riley and I would be dust
under their feet.

How had I done this to my daughter? *How* had I let this
happen?

On top of my own fears, I couldn't stop thinking about the
boy, Blaze. Was he all right? *Please, God, let him live.*

I dragged into the kitchen around 8:30 Sunday morning and slid into my chair with a cup of coffee. In two and a half hours I was scheduled to meet with Eric Chandler. What would I do about that?

My brain barely functioned.

Riley got up around 9:00, slack-faced and lethargic. She slumped in her chair at the kitchen table, unable to eat breakfast. We both still wore our robes.

"Have you heard from anyone how Blaze is doing?" I asked.

"No. I haven't heard from anyone about anything."

Oh, Riley. Not that I was surprised. But *I* should have heard something from Brandon's parents. Hadn't they quizzed him about what I said? Was he still lying to them? If he'd come clean, Morgan and the rest couldn't keep lying. Somewhere in that vetting process Riley and I deserved an apology.

She sighed. "I don't want to go to school tomorrow. Just let me be sick for a few days."

This—again. I wanted to cry for her. "You'll get behind on your studies."

"I don't care."

The clock's hands ticked toward 10:00. If I was going to show up at the Sheriff's headquarters, I should start getting ready. Of course I couldn't really go. If I did, I might not come home again. But if I didn't, Eric Chandler would not let me be. And I'd appear all the more guilty at trying to put him off. Did I want him dragging me away from here in front of Riley?

Inevitability, dark and leaden, would soon pound on my door.

"Riley." I took a deep breath. "I need to go see a Sheriff's deputy at 11:00. They want to ask me some more questions about Paula."

Riley's forehead creased. "Why, what would *you* know?"

I shrugged. "Well, she did come into our office. I guess they just want to ask me more about that. It shouldn't take long."

"Okay." Riley gazed at the table, then wandered off toward her bedroom. So unconcerned. So unsuspecting that she could lose her mother that very day.

My heart broke in two.

As I dressed, denial wriggled into my brain. It was the only means I had left to cope. I'd been wrong about Eric Chandler suspecting me before, hadn't I? So I was wrong again. They just had a few extra questions, that was all. Nothing to worry about. Eric had even wanted to take me out on a date.

Of course, that was before Paula's body had been found.

Still, why wouldn't Eric have arrested me last night if he'd had the evidence?

Maybe because he wanted me to feel at ease. To wander into an interview thinking we were just going to chat about little details he'd overlooked. I would make some stupid mistake—and be caught.

The denial crawled away.

I should call Sam Merilen, the attorney. If I didn't hire the man, J.L. would—as soon as I started talking and accusing *him*. Then both of them would spend their days proving me a liar.

But—me, hire a lawyer? With what money?

The minutes wouldn't stop ticking away. Fate had bolted a chain around my waist and now dragged me toward justice.

The time came for me to leave.

I went to Riley's room to hug her goodbye. Hot tears welled inside me, so deep they didn't reach my eyes. "I love you so much." I could not let her go. "And I'm *so sorry*."

"Mom, don't worry." She patted my back. "I'll be okay."

She thought we were talking about her friends.

I gave her a shaky smile. "Yeah."

My phone's GPS pointed the directions to the Sheriff's headquarters. I drove away from the house, my spine like steel.

You watch crime movies and TV shows, see suspects in those stuffy little interview rooms. A table, a few chairs. Dingy walls, no windows. An invasive, watching camera. You see the person on the hot seat sweat. Lie. His freedom, his *life*, hangs by a thread. We've all witnessed those scenes hundreds of times. But have you ever imagined *yourself* in that situation? Your own life about to be stripped away?

I waited, alone, in the room for ten minutes until Eric Chandler arrived. He carried a sealed manila envelope.

Evidence against me. My dry throat tried to swallow.

"Hi." He gave me a reassuring smile. Didn't fool me. "Sorry to keep you waiting."

I nodded.

He took a seat, laying the envelope on the table. Laced his fingers. So calm. The one in control. "You look nervous."

"I'm just ... my daughter and I had a difficult night last night. She was at a party, and some boy came who'd apparently taken drugs."

"Ah." Eric shook his head. "So many problems with drugs these days. They're everywhere. Our Special Investigations Unit deals with it constantly."

"Did you hear anything about the boy? I just wondered, because doesn't the Sheriff's Office serve Hayden, too? The paramedics came and took him. He wasn't responding."

Realization crossed Eric's face. "Your daughter was at that house? On Hayden Lake?"

"Yes. It really scared her."

"I'll bet."

"Do you know what happened to the boy?"

Eric Chandler gave a slow nod. "I'm sorry to say he didn't make it."

My mouth fell open. "He *died*?"

"On the way to the hospital. They did everything they could, but ... they couldn't resuscitate."

I focused on the floor, feeling sick. That young boy—dead. So young. So much to live for.

"What was his name? I only heard his nickname. Blaze."

"I don't know."

He wasn't just a victim. He had a *name*. "What did he take?"

"Heroin. Injected."

Heroin. How did Morgan get mixed up with a boy like that?

A new thought hit. "Will somebody from the Sheriff's Office be interviewing the kids at that party?"

"Likely, yeah. If any of them happen to know who he bought the drugs from, that would be helpful. Our SIU—the Special Investigations Unit—will go after that person, ultimately trying to work their way up the chain, see who the major supplier is."

Made sense. But being questioned by some deputy would make the kids at that party even more scared. What if they doubled down on their story?

How ironic. I was facing a Sheriff's deputy because of J.L.— and now Riley would face one because of his daughter.

My fingers curled around the edge of my chair. "Well, let me save your special unit some time. Riley, my daughter, didn't know the boy and would have nothing to tell you. She only let him in that house because another girl—Morgan Larrett—asked her to. Apparently he was some secret new boyfriend of Morgan's. And yes, I do mean J.L.'s daughter. She's trying to stay out of trouble by claiming she didn't know him and blaming his presence at the party on Riley. The other kids are backing up Morgan's story because she seems to be a leader in that group." My voice rose. "But Riley knows nothing. She's a new kid at that school, and she's been bullied enough. I will not have you questioning her and upsetting her all the more."

I glared at Deputy Chandler, knowing my cheeks were too red and my tone too strident. I didn't care.

He raised a shoulder, his expression unchanging. "Okay. I'll let them know."

Just like that. I leaned back in my seat.

If only it could be so simple with me. "Thank you."

Eric pulled his notebook and pen out of his pocket. Wrote something down and circled it. "J.L.'s daughter, huh." He made a *tsk* sound through his teeth. "Kids. Raising them is never easy."

"True." I gazed at the notebook. Would he write in it as he questioned me?

I raked in a steadying breath.

Eric patted the table. "All right. Let's get down to the reason I asked you here." He shifted in his chair. "Just wanted to go over a few things. First, remember I asked you what color sweater Paula was wearing? You said you couldn't recall."

"I guess it was red."

"You guess?"

"Well, I ... that's what I read in a newspaper article. So now when I picture her in J.L.'s office, I see her sweater as red."

"But that's only because of the article? You can't be certain in your own mind?"

What should I say? He was walking me into a trap.

My head shook. "I guess not. I really don't know."

He made a note. "I talked to Margie Stohl—remember, the woman you met who works across the street at the cleaners? She told me Paula's sweater was blue."

She *did?* So she'd lied to me, claiming she only saw the white scarf as "Paula" drove away. Did Margie suspect me even then?

An oily mass rolled through my stomach.

"Do you remember it being blue?"

"No. I really don't remember the color."

"Okay." Eric made another note. "Just for the record—when we found her body, the sweater was red." He eyed me, awaiting my response.

"Oh." I shrugged. "I guess Margie just remembered it wrong."

"Yeah. That can happen."

"Yeah."

He regarded me a moment longer. "You clearly remembered a scarf, however."

"Yes. White. She had it on her head when she left."

"Okay." More writing. "Anything more you can add to that?"

I frowned at the table. "Don't think so."

"All right. What time did Paula leave your office?"

He'd already asked me these questions. Was he asking them again to see if I'd change my story?

"I think it was around 4:30."

"Uh-huh."

And he continued writing in that notebook of his. What for? Wasn't the camera capturing all this anyway?

"Did Vince Rayle happen to call that afternoon?"

I cocked my head. "I ... don't think so."

"Would you remember if he'd called?"

"I remember he called the next day. In the morning."

"But not the day before. The day you saw Paula."

"No."

Eric nodded. "What did Mr. Rayle say when he called the following day?"

"He was really irritated. He wanted to know if Paula had come to see J.L. the day before, because by then she was missing."

"And what did you tell him?"

"I didn't tell him anything. I just put him through to J.L. Then later that day—maybe in the afternoon?—Mr. Rayle came to the office. Sounded just as mad as before. Maybe he always sounds that way."

"What did he say at that time?"

"He demanded to see J.L. Said he didn't have—and didn't need—an appointment. And he was complaining about you, and all the questions you were asking him about Paula."

"Okay." Eric Chandler kept a poker face. "Anything else?"

"I didn't hear anything. He went into J.L.'s office, and they closed the door."

Why all these questions about Vince Rayle?

Eric sat back in his chair. "Just curious—why do you think Mr. Rayle would come to J.L. about all this?"

"I don't know. Well, the phone call—that apparently was to check if it was true that Paula had shown up there the day before. But why he'd come to the office in person to complain about you, I don't know."

Eric looked away for a moment. "Are he and J.L. close?"

"I have no idea. I've only been at my job for two weeks."

Two weeks. It seemed like an eternity.

"To your knowledge, has Mr. Rayle called or come to the office since Wednesday?"

"Yes. He called on Friday."

"What time was that?"

"Late in the afternoon. He'd heard that Paula's roommate had identified her body. That's how J.L. found out."

"I see. Okay."

Eric Chandler tapped his pen against the table. He gazed at his notes for a moment, then looked me in the eye. "There's something I want to show you." He gestured with his chin toward the envelope.

My body went cold.

The deputy leaned back in his chair and pulled a pair of latex gloves from his pocket. Slid them on. If he was going for dramatic effect, it was working. I watched in crushed silence, my throat slowly closing.

He stuck his gloved hand in the envelope and pulled out something long and white. Laid it on the table before me.

"Recognize this scarf?"

CHAPTER 34

Riley lolled around on her bed. What to do with herself? Her mom wasn't even home. And the silence on her phone was killing her. Not a single text from anybody. What did that mean? Were they mad? Still blaming her? Or just busy doing other things?

But she should be hearing something. Like—what happened to Blaze in the hospital? Didn't anybody care how he was doing?

Well *she* cared. She picked up her phone and texted Morgan.

HOW IS BLAZE?

Riley clutched her cell, watching the screen.
No answer.

U OKAY MORGAN?

Nothing.

Riley bit her lip. Why would Morgan shut her out? She'd let Blaze into the party, like Morgan wanted. And when everything went wrong and they all played innocent, she hadn't ratted on them.

But her mom had said things to Brandon. Maybe he told Morgan.

Riley texted Alissa, then Bella, then Lauren. Had they heard from Morgan? Did they know how Blaze was doing?

No reply. Not one.

Riley's chin sank. This couldn't be happening again.

She rolled onto her stomach and pounded her pillow. This had to be because of what her mom said to Brandon and his parents. By now, everyone had likely heard about it. They'd all group against her more than ever. Morgan, in her sugar-sweetest way, would swear she'd never even seen Blaze before. And Alissa, Lauren, and Bella could say they'd never heard her talk about him, because that was true. Didn't matter what they *knew* in their hearts. They all had too much to lose. And Riley was just the new girl, so who cared?

If she lost Morgan as a friend, would Mr. Larrett stop paying her tuition? Riley squeezed her eyes closed. Then she'd have to go back to Payton Middle.

She would run away before that happened.

In fact, she and her mom needed to leave this town. Start over somewhere else—

Her phone pinged. Riley sat up. A text from Morgan.

WHY SHOULD I KNOW HOW BLAZE IS.
I DON'T KNOW HIM. UR THE ONE WHO
LET HIM IN THE PARTY.

Bees swarmed in Riley's head. She dropped the phone and slapped her hands over her face.

Morgan was through with her. And there was nothing she could do. Cross-legged, Riley rocked and rocked. Her eyes couldn't even cry anymore.

You could make this go away.

The words floated into her brain.

Riley stopped moving and stared across the room, thinking.

That's what Morgan wanted, wasn't it—her to take the blame for what happened. Say she'd met Blaze around town and invited him to the party. Riley may never be allowed back at Brandon's house, but Morgan and all the others would be her friends again. Maybe they'd like her even more—because she'd covered for them.

Riley plucked at her bedspread. Yeah, and everything would be great—until the next time Morgan needed something from her. How many times would Riley have to lie? Do things she didn't want to do?

What kind of friendship was that?

Still, it would be better than being shunned. Better than going back to Payton Middle.

Riley stared at her phone. Slowly she picked it up. Three times she started to text, then stopped.

She threw her cell on the bed.

Her mom would want her to be strong. Stand up for herself. Ever since Mom had gotten a divorce from Riley's dad, that's what *she* had tried to do.

But Riley wasn't that strong.

She heaved a sigh and picked up her phone. Her fingers dragged as she texted Morgan.

> UR RIGHT. REALLY SORRY I LET HIM
> IN. PLEASE FORGIVE.

Riley held her breath.
Her screen lit up.

> DON'T WORRY ABOUT IT.

Yes! Riley flopped onto her back in relief. As she held her cell above her head, a second text appeared.

> WANT 2 COME OVER?

CHAPTER 35

Paula's scarf.

How—?

I stared at the soiled white fabric, mind spiraling. "It looks like the scarf Paula was wearing. It wasn't dirty like that, though." Amazingly, my voice remained even. "Is that it?"

"Quite possibly."

"What do you mean? Was she wearing it when you found her?"

"No. It was in a dumpster. We got an anonymous tip."

A tip? *No.* Some person saw J.L. throw the scarf and purse in there?

A realization struck me broadside. Was that why Eric was asking questions about J.L.?

"A *dumpster*? Oh."

"Yeah. So I wondered if you could identify it."

"I see." I leaned forward, frowning at the scarf. "Best I can tell, it's the same one. Could it have fingerprints on it?"

No response.

My nerves sizzled. How to cover myself? "Well, if it happens to have mine, I guess you *will* know it's hers."

Surprise flickered across Eric's face. "Are your prints on file?"

"Oh." A voice in my head screamed. *Why* had I said that? Now it was too late to backtrack. "Guess not. No reason for them to be."

My heart flailed. I did not know how to do this. I was caught. Nailed to the wall.

"Why would they be on the scarf?" Eric tilted his head.

Lies jammed into my mouth. "'Cause I took it from Paula when she came in. I usually take clients' coats and things and hang them up on the antler tree. She didn't have a coat, though."

"So you hung up her scarf for her?"

"Yes. Gave it back to her when she left. That's why I remembered so well how she put it on—over her head, I mean."

Eric scratched his jaw. "You said she was really angry when she arrived, correct?"

"Yes."

"But she stopped to give you her scarf?"

My nerves thrummed. Another misstep. Plus, now I had the scarf hanging on the antler tree instead of in J.L.'s office. What if *his* prints were on it? How to explain that?

"Well, I offered to take it. I was trying to be nice, you know, in the midst of her rudeness."

"Sure. Okay."

We both stared at the scarf. My hands tremored. I dropped them into my lap.

Eric tapped a gloved finger against the table. "Anything else you can think of?"

"No."

"All right."

My palms were wet. I rubbed them against my jeans, watching in torment as Eric slipped the scarf back into the envelope.

He laid it aside and took off the gloves.

What about the purse? J.L. had thrown it in the dumpster, too. Maybe they *had* found it.

Of course they had. Along with Paula's cell phone inside. With the battery removed. Somewhere, on something, they'd lifted an unidentified fingerprint. One of mine I hadn't wiped clean.

Dread smeared through my stomach. I couldn't take much more.

"Are we done? I need to get back to Riley."

Eric sat back in his chair. "If you don't mind, I'd like to take your fingerprints before you go."

The words muddled in my brain. Fingerprints ... Before you go ...

He was going to let me walk *out* of there?

"I—I need to get home. Can't you wait to see if you need them?"

"Quicker for our investigation if you do it now."

I studied the table. Would he still let me go if I refused?

This is why he'd brought me down here, wasn't it—to get my prints. No matter that I could leave now. As soon as they matched me to something in Paula's purse—it was over.

"Let's go get it done." Eric Chandler stood.

I struggled to my feet, hands gripping the table. Surely he could see my guilt.

The process didn't take long, my fingertips deduced to perfect prints. My calling cards. The stark evidence left behind that would betray me.

Eric Chandler was done with me. I felt chewed up and spit out. On wobbly ankles, I made my way toward the building's exit, pulled by the freedom, however brief, that awaited.

As I started the car, a wild thought slammed me—grab Riley and run. To the other end of the country, as far away as we could. We'd drive to the southern tip of Florida. Change our names, dye our hair—

My cell phone went off. Riley's ringtone.

My hand scrambled inside my purse to pull out the phone. "Hi, I'm in the car."

"Okay, but—"

"I'll be home soon."

"Wait, Mom!"

"What *is* it?" My fingers clenched the wheel, my heart skidding. I could barely breathe. There could be no running—they'd only find me. I had to stay here and do something to save myself. Today, before it was too late.

"What's wrong with you, Mom?"

"Nothing, what do you want?"

"You don't have to get all mad. I just want to know if you can take me to Morgan's this afternoon?"

The question cut right through me. The very mention of J.L.'s daughter's name …

"*Why* would you want to go to her house?" My voice was too harsh, but I couldn't stop. "With all the lies she's telling about you?"

"We're okay now."

"Really. Has she told the truth about Blaze?"

"No."

"*No?*"

Were any of the kids even aware he'd died? Riley couldn't know yet, or she'd be upset.

"So what are you going to do, Riley? Just let her continue in this scheming charade at your expense?"

"I … don't know."

"Well, *what* then?"

Riley stuttered in air. "I just want friends, Mom." The words collapsed on themselves.

Quick tears bit my eyes. Oh, Riley. How could this happen to her? She was *so* letting herself be used.

My voice softened. "Look, let's just … I'm driving right now. I'll be home in ten minutes. We'll talk about this when I get there. All right?"

A long pause. "Yeah." She sniffed.

"Okay, sit tight. See you soon." I ended the call.

No way was she going to Morgan Larrett's house that day. Or ever.

When I pulled into our garage, I shut off the car, then sat immobilized. What to do now? Warn Riley that law enforcement would be at our door before the day was over?

How could I possibly tell her that?

The car soon turned cold. Still I hung there, my hands on the wheel with nowhere to go. Memories of my life struggles—the abuse in my childhood and marriage, my husband's betrayal and divorce, my wild hope at starting over—swelled and boiled and crashed over me. How often I'd been the helpless victim. How much I'd wanted to change that in Payton—for myself and for Riley.

I had so miserably failed.

The door to the house opened. Riley poked her head out. "Mom? You coming in?"

I sucked in a despairing breath and nodded.

In the kitchen, feeling ragged and worn, I set my purse on the table and faced Riley. "Let's sit down, okay?"

Fright veiled her face. "What is it? What's wrong?"

"Sit." I pulled out my chair.

She took a seat across from me.

"I ... have sad news. About Blaze. I heard today that he died on the way to the hospital."

"What? *No.*" Riley's face crumpled.

"I'm so sorry." I stretched out my hand to cover hers as she cried.

"I didn't see him take any drugs, Mom, really." Her chest shuddered. "If I had, maybe I could've done something ..."

"Riley, this is not your fault. He shot up with heroin before going to that party. There is absolutely nothing you could have done. Even the paramedics couldn't save him."

She gazed at the table and nodded. A tear fell off her jaw and splatted on the wood.

I squeezed her fingers. "Now listen. This situation of lying about who knew Blaze—that's about to go to a whole new level. Law enforcement people need to know who sold him the drugs. They may want to question kids at the party. Morgan and the others might lie to Brandon's parents, but I'm hoping they won't lie to a deputy."

Riley's eyes widened. "If they think *I* knew him—"

"They don't. I've already taken care of that. I told a deputy if the kids claim Blaze was your friend, they're lying."

Riley soaked that in. "Did you tell him it was Morgan?"

"Mm-hmm."

"You *did?*"

"Yes."

Riley dropped her head in her hands. "They'll *never* be my friends now." The words muffled.

I pressed back in my chair, throat aching as she sniffed and cried.

She raised up, her eyes red and lips twisted. "How could you *do* this to me?"

That question dug so much deeper than she could imagine.

"What else could I do? Just let their lies stand? Let some deputy question you and not believe *your* statements?"

"I ... no."

"What then?"

"I don't know."

"I'm trying to protect you, Riley."

She looked away at nothing. Swiped her cheek. "I want to be protected and have friends, too."

"I know. I really do understand. But you can't control what they do. You can only control what *you* do. And if they choose to lie, cheat, steal, whatever—you can't sit back and let them blame it on you. Believe me, you let them get away with one thing, they'll do it again. You'll be their doormat. You think that's what real friendship looks like?"

She shook her head.

"Morgan started this. Not you."

Riley looked down. Rubbed a thumb over her other hand. "*You've* done it."

"Done what?"

"Let people treat you bad. Like Dad."

The accusation seared my lungs.

"He did it for years."

My eyes welled. Riley glanced up and saw them. Her mouth opened—for an apology?—but no words came.

"I wanted to teach you differently, Riley. I don't want you to make the same mistakes I did. Now we're on our own, where we should be. And we can do better."

She swallowed. "But *you* didn't leave." Her voice cracked. "Dad did."

True.

"And if he hadn't, maybe we'd still be there."

I raised a shoulder. "But we're not. And now we're trying to live more productive lives. You didn't like what you saw between me and your dad. I know that. Marriage is a lot harder to deal with than friendship. If you don't like what you saw in that situation, don't do the same thing in yours. Learn from my mistakes."

Riley tipped her head back to stare at the ceiling. "I want to. I just … right now—what that looks like? It scares me."

Pain burst in my chest. Such honest wisdom from my thirteen-year-old.

When I was arrested and spilled the story of what J.L. had forced me to do, if no one else believed me, Riley would. But how could I ever look her in the eye?

My cell phone rang. Riley and I both jumped.

Sighing, I pulled it from my purse. The caller ID read *J.L. Larrett.*

My skin pebbled. Why would he be calling now?

He knew something. Maybe he knew Eric Chandler was on his way to arrest me.

"I'd better take this." I rose. "I'll be right back."

My finger tapped on *talk* as I headed toward the bedroom. "Hello?"

"Hi." J.L.'s voice pulsed with … something. Satisfaction? "I'm officially calling about what happened at the kids' party. In case anyone should ever ask."

Officially? "Okay."

"What I'm really calling about is Paula's murder."

I shut the bedroom door and wilted onto my bed. "Yes?"

"They've got their suspect."

My throat caved in.

"They just arrested Vince Rayle."

CHAPTER 36

J .L.'s words would not gel in my brain. I clutched the phone, struggling for a reply. "What did you say?"

"You heard me. Vince Rayle. They got him."

"What? How ...?"

"They arrested him, Cara. He's in jail. And probably won't get bail."

My spine melted. I slumped over, dragging in air. Intense relief gushed over me like a river exploding its banks.

"I hear they got a lot of evidence against him."

How? The evidence all pointed to *me*.

I straightened, the relief draining away. J.L. was playing me. Or this was a trap. Maybe he was taping the call.

I needed to choose my words carefully.

"What evidence? And how do you know?"

"I've got friends down in the Sheriff's Office, you know that."

I waited.

"I'll tell you what I know, but you got to keep it to yourself. That's very important, Cara."

"Yes. Okay."

"For one thing, they found Paula's scarf in a dumpster around the corner from Vince's house."

I pictured Eric Chandler, the scarf on the table between us. "That's not proof he did it."

"No, but it was suspicious. Plus, remember the fingerprint they found in the backseat of Paula's car? It's Vince's."

Vince's? Not mine? "Are you telling me the truth?"

"Of course! You think I'm making this up?"

Was he?

Why would he? If he was taping this call, if some deputy was listening, I could blurt out any moment that J.L. was the real killer. He wouldn't place himself in such an uncontrolled situation.

The fingerprint was *not mine*.

I shoved a fist against my cheek. "That's not enough, either. Paula was his girlfriend. He could have been in that car many times."

J.L. chuckled. "How about finding her purse, with her cell phone inside, hidden in his closet?"

My jaw unhinged.

"Got you there, didn't I."

"I … I don't understand."

"The purse was wrapped in a towel that had a spot of blood on it. That blood's gonna come back to Vince. Poor guy must have cut himself shaving."

I stared at the worn carpet, processing the ramifications of such evidence. "But how did the purse get there?"

"Obviously he hid it. Why he didn't throw it in the dumpster, too, I don't know. Maybe it had to do with the money in her wallet, or the phone."

J.L. told me he'd thrown *everything* in that dumpster. The scarf, the purse, the cell ...

"There's more. They found a house key up on the cliff in the forest. You know, where Paula's body would have been thrown off. That key fit Vince's front door."

What?

A cog inside my brain vibrated, then slowly clunked into place. Creaking gears turned. I saw myself *rifling through Paula's purse, her body at my feet. "See that big house key?" J.L. points to a large gold one. "Doesn't belong to her. Put it on the table." He wipes it off with a tissue. Drops both items in his pocket ...*

"Tell me how that key would have gotten there, Cara. Up on that cliff."

No response could form in my throat.

"Cara." J.L.'s voice hardened. "Tell me how that key got there."

All this time, everything J.L. had done. And I hadn't understood the half of it.

"Do we need to talk about this more tomorrow at the office? Maybe I need to review your first two weeks on the job."

Now he was threatening to fire me? Would his manipulation never end?

"You *better* talk to me."

Rusty air seeped through my lungs. "I guess ... when ... Vince got rid of Paula's body, it fell out of his pocket."

"Yes! Very good."

Such taunt in those words.

"You need to say that, *think* that, until the words feel right, know what I mean?"

They would never feel right.

"You're free, Cara. See? I *told* you I'd take care of you. You and Riley both. There's no need to worry anymore."

Free.

How I longed for wild relief to pour over me again. I needed it to wash away the riddling fear. Make me whole, light. I closed my eyes and called the relief back. Begged for it. But a brittle wind came instead, one that would shrink me to nothing.

An innocent man was going to jail in our place.

J.L. made a sound in his throat. "Am I gonna hear a thank you?"

But this didn't make sense. Why had Eric interrogated me?

"Deputy Chandler showed up here last night and insisted on questioning me. I went down there this morning. He showed me the scarf—"

"*We got an anonymous tip* ... "

My breath caught.

"*You* called in that tip, didn't you."

He chuckled. "Vince shouldn't have been dumb enough to use a dumpster so close to his house."

My fingers cramped around the phone. I could hardly believe this. When had J.L. planned it all? "Doesn't Vince have an alibi for that night? I thought he was at his cabin."

"He lied. He was in Payton. That's what made them start suspecting him in the first place."

But how had J.L. known Vince would lie? "So why would Deputy Chandler want my fingerprints? I thought he was going to match them to ones found on the scarf."

"On the scarf? No. Very hard to get prints off fabric. There are ways to do it, and sometimes it works, but it's expensive. Not something our Sheriff's Office would typically try."

"How do you know that?"

"I just do."

Of course he did. Or he'd never have called in the tip.

"But Eric Chandler *told* me they'd found prints."

"Did he? Or did he just lead you to think that?"

He *had* said it. Hadn't he? But I'd been in such a rush to explain why my prints might be on the scarf. "Why would he be questioning me at all if they were preparing to arrest Vince?"

"Eric's a good lawman. He was just trying to fill any holes in the case. Believe me, if he'd wanted to corner you on something, he would have. Besides, he got more evidence on Vince after he showed up at your house last night. They found the purse and matched the key this morning. I'll bet Eric ended up asking more questions about Vince than you."

Air pushed from my mouth. J.L. was right.

I forced myself off the bed. Shuffled to the window. "The hunter who found Paula—was that you, too?"

"Really, Cara. It's deer season. Hunters are all over those woods. It was just a matter of time."

"Animals will find her before any human does." J.L.'s words to me.

"You *knew* she'd be found?"

I thought of her car, left so close to Highway 95. Where someone would spot it within hours.

So ... all this time, J.L. had been planning to frame Vince? Had J.L. stood in his office, her body at his feet, already scheming? He'd just needed me to help him get rid of the body. And as a back-up fall guy, in case the frame job on Vince didn't work. Either way, the one person who'd never be held accountable for Paula's death was J.L.

I leaned my forehead against the cold glass.

"Nice talking to you, Cara, I need to go," J.L. said. "Just wanted you to know all this. Now it's done. You don't have to be afraid. Just *say nothing.* Understand?"

Forever this guilt would weigh on me. *Forever.*

"*Do* you?"

"Yes."

"Good. If you should be called to testify at Vince's trial, no worries. It'll just be the same questions Eric already asked you. All right?"

Sure. No worries. "Okay."

"That's my girl."

My eyes squeezed shut.

"I gotta say—I thought you'd be more grateful."

What this man had done to me. Had made me. I hated him.

"I *am* grateful."

"Good. So act like it."

A hysterical laugh bounced around inside me. "Give me time."

"Cara. I've just given you the rest of your life."

CHAPTER 37

The line went dead. I lowered the phone, my thoughts whirlpooling.

I worked for a monster. Killing wasn't enough. Vince Rayle was supposed to be J.L.'s friend.

If he could do that to a friend and client, what would he do to me if I ever talked?

Numbness chewed my legs. I needed to move. Take the next step in this life J.L. had given me.

Riley. I stumbled toward the door. My reflection in the dresser mirror caught my eye.

I swung away.

As I left the bedroom I remembered J.L. had mentioned the kids' party. Did he even know Blaze had died? Not that he would care.

Did he know Blaze was Morgan's boyfriend?

J.L. was being played, too. At my daughter's expense.

My fingers curled into my palms.

Riley sat on the couch, watching TV. "What took you so long?" I tried to smile. "Sorry. It was … just about work."

Her eyes widened. "Morgan's dad?"

"Yeah." I sat down beside her.

"Is he mad at me because of the party? Is he gonna stop paying for my school?"

My heart cracked. I pulled her close. "No."

"You sure?"

"I'm sure."

She wriggled out of my arms and sat up straight. "Okay then, I've decided something."

"Yeah?"

Riley licked her lips. "I'm not gonna let Morgan lie about me. Like what you and I talked about. I'm gonna tell the truth. And if she doesn't like me anymore …." Riley clutched her hands together. "Well, then she's not worth being my friend."

Tears scratched my eyes. I was not worthy of my own daughter. Her forehead creased. "I didn't mean to make you cry."

"I know." My throat ached. "I'm just so proud of you. And things will get better, you'll see. People will respect you in the end."

She leaned against my side, and I put an arm around her. We sat there for some time, my fingers stroking her hair. Sobs wailed within me, but I caged them between my ribs. At least no one would snatch me away from my daughter now. I could stay by her side, mother her, be there throughout all her joys and hurts. Be her role model.

Don't laugh. I know.

Riley did not go to Morgan's that afternoon. Instead I took her to a movie. A comedy. What better way to spend the afternoon that stretched before us? To purge my mind? I bought the theater's ridiculously expensive popcorn, and we shared a soft drink. We laughed and stuffed ourselves until our fingers were slick with butter. On the way home we bought fast food, which we ate on the couch, watching TV. Not the healthiest diet that day.

I thought I'd lacked sleep before. That night it was worse than ever. I tossed in bed, thinking of everything and nothing. What to look forward to but Monday? Working for a man who chained me. Whose daughter tried to chain mine.

How could I let Riley visit J.L.'s house? Be friends with Morgan?

Could I ever hoard enough money to move away? I had no savings. And my house lease tied me for a full year.

Would J.L. ever *let* me go?

Details of the case floated in and out of my head. How had J.L. gotten Paula's purse into Vince's closet? When? Had he used that key? Then *gone back* into the forest to drop it?

More than once that wild thought pummeled me—grab Riley and run. But with what money? And if I did run, J.L. would not just let me alone. I'd be too much of a liability. Out there, somewhere, knowing the truth. He'd pay someone to track me down. And I'd be dead, too. Just like Paula.

He had encased my future in concrete. I had no way out.

Nothing left to do but pray.

MONDAY, NOVEMBER 20

CHAPTER 38

On Monday Riley begged me to let her stay home from school. Determined as she'd been to take the high ground with Morgan, when it came right down to it, she wasn't ready.

Given my own lack of courage, who was I to tell her no? I called the school.

"Keep the doors locked," I told her on the way out. Time for me to go to work. And serve J.L.

"I always do, Mom."

The ride to work was cold. I'd forgotten my coat.

When I reached the office, the morning paper lay outside the door—which meant J.L. hadn't arrived yet. I could see the headline above the fold. "Arrest in Tellinger Murder."

I swept up the paper and threw it on my desk. It pulled at me as I hurried through making J.L.'s coffee.

In my chair I hunched over, devouring the article. It did not mention details of the case against Vince Rayle. It only quoted

Deputy Eric Chandler saying the evidence against him was "strong" and they were "sure they had the right man."

I fell back in my chair, chilled and empty. How I wished I could rejoice.

J.L. arrived. I could not bring myself to even say hello.

"Well, good morning to you, too, Cara." He had a new jaunt in his step as he headed for the coffee machine, humming under his breath. "Ah, smells great."

He knew I watched as he poured himself a cup. A miasma of self-satisfaction hung about him. How did this man live in his own skin?

J.L. set down the coffee pot, irritation flicking across his face. "What are you looking at?"

What, indeed.

"I just want to know why you did this. Why Vince Rayle?"

J.L. heaved a martyr's sigh. "Cara, that is done. I do *not* want to discuss it. Right now you and I have other things to talk about."

"But he's innocent. "

J.L.'s expression turned to stone. He thumped down his mug on the coffee table, sloshing liquid. In three strides he crossed to tower over me, rage narrowing his eyes. "Where's your cell phone?"

I gazed up at him, cowering. "What?"

"Your phone. Give it to me."

"I—it's in my purse."

J.L. thrust out his hand.

Heart hammering, I fumbled in my handbag for the phone. Dropped it into his palm.

He examined it. Pressed the button to turn on its screen. "Unlock it."

I obeyed. He grabbed it back. "It's not taping?"

"What? *No.*"

J.L. threw the cell down. "You wired?" He jumped around the desk and yanked me from my chair.

"Stop!"

He pinned me with one arm and ran heavy fingers over my back. Then felt my chest.

I struggled against his grasp. "Get off me!"

Satisfied, he pushed me away. I stumbled back, gasping and violated. My cheeks burned.

"Sorry." J.L. adjusted his clothes. "Had to be sure."

I collapsed into my chair, tears in my eyes.

"Cara. I'm sorry, okay?"

My head shook. How *dare* he?

"Stop now." His voice tightened. "Enough. I had to make sure I could trust you."

"What have I done to make you think you can't?" The words choked. "I've done *everything* you said."

"Okay, okay." He held up both hands.

I leaned over my desk, stuttering in air.

J.L. picked up my cell, still unlocked, and tapped in a number. I had no strength to even ask who he was calling.

Filtering through the phone, a man's voice answered. "Yeah."

"Code Hawaii."

"Who are you?"

"A friend of Vince's. He's still in jail."

"I heard. I don't like workin' with people I don't know."

"You got no choice tonight."

"I want assurance. Understand?"

"You'll get it. Call you back."

J.L. tapped off the call.

My brain barely registered the conversation. I folded my arms in a self-hug. If only I could crawl into a hole. Another man's hands on me. More abuse. When would this ever stop in my life?

J.L. made a point of carefully setting down my phone. "Vince is not the perfect citizen, if it makes you feel any better, Cara. He played me. Bad. Pulled me into a world I didn't want to be in. For the last four years he's had me where he wanted me. And I had no way to escape."

Sounded familiar. And here it came again—the speech. Something to make me feel sorry for J.L. Larrett. Make me think him more human.

He moved closer to my desk. Stuck a hand in his pocket. "It started when Morgan was so sick. Vince had this new trucking company. So I started doing taxes for it, like I'd been doing for Vince's construction. I made a dumb mistake, I'll admit it. People in my line of work—we take courses that train us to spot money laundering. Vince had been my client for so long, I wasn't paying enough attention. Should have. He's never been the straightest shooter." J.L. paused. "You listening, Cara? This is going to be very important to you."

I was still bent over my desk. My head nodded.

"Turned out a lot of what that trucking business does is launder drug money. Not an easy thing to do, turn all that cash into valid funds in a bank. He hides the cash under fake floors in his trucks, then takes product loads for some client across the Canadian border. The trucking business is legit, and he pays taxes on that income. But the hidden cash is unpacked on the other side and run through banks. I didn't know the laundering part until it was too late. Vince even claimed more and more income on the legit side every year—that he paid taxes on—just to have on record in case he was ever investigated as to where he got all his money.

When I found out what he was doing, I said I wanted no part of it. But he threatened me. He could have exposed me. I'd have lost my business. Gone to jail. Just at the time all those medical bills were coming due. Ever since then, Vince has held this over my head. And I've had to help him continue doing it."

I hadn't moved, focusing on the grains in the wood of my desk.

"See, Cara? Vince has no idea who killed Paula. And now that he's in jail, he has no reason to tell anyone how I helped him launder money. That would only implicate *him*. Add more years to his prison sentence. I've cleaned everything up. Brilliantly. I can keep my business. And you can keep your job. If I'd gone down, you wouldn't survive a month without income. You and Riley would be out on the street."

Of course. All of this was for *me*.

Slowly, I straightened. "I have a hard time believing Vince Rayle *made* you do anything. I'll bet he paid you out of his cut of that laundered money." I'd seen the claimed income on Vince Rayle's tax documents. It was probably a pittance compared to the illegal money he'd made.

J.L. glared at me. "I had bills to pay. I had a family to think of, just like you. Once Morgan was well, I was stuck. Think of the things *you've* done in the last week—for *your* daughter. Where would Riley be without you if you went to prison?"

And who had put me in this position?

J.L. flexed his shoulders. "Think what Vince did to me, Cara. He pulled me into *international drug trafficking*. I couldn't stop what I was doing. I couldn't tell anybody what I knew. That's a good way to get yourself and your whole family killed. After four years I'd had enough of it. I had to find a way out."

Find a way out. The words sank into me. Wait. When? *When* had he decided this?

A stunning thought pressed me against the back of my chair. Could this be right? Had I been that much of a puppet? All this time?

I gazed up at J.L., searching for breath to speak. Feeling my heart in a death flutter. Even before I asked the question, I knew where the answer would lead. "Did Paula know about the money laundering?"

J.L. made a face. "Vince would never tell her that."

Of course not. I pictured Paula, barging into our office, demanding to see J.L. She'd been his puppet, too, hadn't she.

A fist curled inside my stomach.

I swallowed. "So how'd you get her to come here, J.L.? Last Tuesday, when she stormed in, so mad. Surely you didn't call her. That would leave a phone record."

J.L.'s eyes hooded. His tongue moved around under his top lip. "Think you're smart, don't you." The words fell like lead.

Smart? No. I was the biggest patsy alive.

All those days I thought I was building a new life for myself and Riley ….

I lowered my head, my voice catching. "Just give me the truth, you owe me that. I can't tell anyone. I just want to know." Tears stung my eyes. "When you interviewed me over the phone, had you planned it all then?"

Had he wanted someone broken, a single mother, needy and alone with her child, for the job? Someone who sounded victimized. Who'd easily cave …

J.L. chuckled in his throat. "Cara. Dear woman. You always were the perfect one for this job."

I pulled my hands together in my lap. Watched one blurry thumb rub over the other. A scene of Riley filled my mind. Sitting at home, alone, afraid to go back to school with this man's daughter. Trusting me with her life.

"And now, Cara, you've got one more thing to do for me. For us. Then you're done—and free forever. I promise."

I barely heard the words.

"Look at me. *Listen.*"

My head weighed a thousand pounds. I struggled to raise it. J.L. stood with one hand on his hip, his mouth in a hard line.

"One last shipment of cash has to go out in Vince's trucks tonight. He's in jail. That leaves *you* to meet with his client and get the money packed."

CHAPTER 39

H EY WHAT ' S WRONG WITH U . R U
REALLY SICK .

The text from Morgan flicked onto Riley's phone as she lay
on the sofa, watching TV.

Riley stared at the words. How to answer? This was a new
day. Would Morgan decide to be her friend today—or not?

Her phone pinged again.

I HEARD THAT GUY U LET IN
THE PARTY DIED . U MUST FEEL
TERRIBLE .

And again.

B RANDON ' S MOM KNOWS U LIED ABOUT
KNOWING HIM . M AYBE IF U SAY

SORRY 2 HER SHE'LL LET U COME TO
HIS NEXT PARTY WHENEVER HE HAS
1.

A fourth text.

HOPE UR NOT 2 SICK. MISS SEEING
U. WE'LL HAVE FUN TOMORROW.
MAYBE U CAN COME OVER 2 MY HOUSE
AFTER SCHOOL.

Riley threw down her phone. Morgan Larrett didn't even care that Blaze was *dead.* All she cared about was keeping the blame off herself.

She was an awful person. Riley wished she never had to see her again.

Riley pushed off the couch and went into the kitchen. She needed something to do. Anything to take her mind off Morgan, this new great "friend." Who would stay her friend forever. And whose father would keep paying for Riley's school tuition. As long as she was willing to sell her own soul.

She flopped into a kitchen chair. Gazed around.

Maybe she should bake cookies. Look up a new recipe from Pinterest.

Her cell pinged again.

Riley swung her head toward the sound. She didn't want to see the new text. But the phone pulled at her.

Heaving a sigh, she headed back to the living room and picked up the phone. Tapped in her code.

U R GOING 2 ANSWER ME. RIGHT?

Riley squinched up her face. She sat down hard on the sofa, a fist digging into her chin.

"I hate my life."

The words bounced around the dull walls.

She rubbed her cheek. Finger-combed her hair. The cell felt heavy in her hand.

Yesterday she'd told her mom she would stand up for herself. Her mom would be so ashamed of her if she didn't.

But her mom wasn't the one who had to go to school and face Morgan.

Riley threw down the cell and punched the sofa cushion. Twice. A third time. Then sighed again—and picked up the phone.

Tomorrow. She could stand up for herself then.

Yeah. Tomorrow.

Riley felt the bend of her back as she hunched over to type.

HI. JUST AWAY FROM THE PHONE 4 A MINUTE. NOT 2 SICK. B BETTER TOMORROW. SEE U THEN.

CHAPTER 40

I stared at J.L., feeling my jaw loosen. A shipment of cash? Was that what the phone call was about?

He spread his hands. "It'll be easy. A quick meeting. Len packs the trucks, and you're out of there."

"Len?"

"The guy in charge, the one I just called. Your contact."

The drug seller. *My* contact?

I closed my eyes, seeking strength within myself. Whatever J.L. was trying to do to me this time—I couldn't allow it.

"J.L. No."

"You don't have a choice."

"Why don't *you* go?"

He smiled. "Cara. Really."

Of course he wouldn't. He wanted me as his fall guy. Again. Someone to be caught red-handed if things went awry.

I pulled in a deep breath. Let it out. "Why does this have to be done, anyway? Vince is in jail. It's over."

"Just one more time, then it *will* be over."

"*Why?*"

"Like I said, Vince doesn't suspect me. He has no idea I put him behind bars. And right now he thinks he'll get out in a day or two—as soon as the Sheriff's Office realizes they've made a mistake. He doesn't know the evidence they have against him. He'll find out soon enough. In the meantime, a shipment needs to be packed tonight. Happens every six days."

Every six days? I calculated back to the past Tuesday, when Paula had been murdered.

Six days ago.

Understanding sank in. *That* was how J.L. had known Vince would have no alibi that night. At least none he could tell law enforcement.

"You need to do this, Cara. Vince expects me to take care of it. Cover for him until he gets out of jail. If I don't, he'll wonder why. He may start to suspect me. And *that* would involve you."

"He expects *you* to take care of it, not me. Why would he want me to know about all this?"

"He wouldn't. But he'll never know you went instead of me. Because by tomorrow or the next day he's gonna have much worse problems. He's about to learn he's stuck in jail on an airtight murder charge."

I looked away, shaking my head.

"Vince saw his attorney yesterday after his arrest. Sam Merilen. A client of mine—you met him. Vince sent me a message through Sam—to handle it. Included the code word, Hawaii. Sam has no idea what the message means. Besides, he's bound by attorney/client privilege not to say anything."

I pushed my chair away from the desk. "I don't care about any code word. I don't care about *any* of this. You're doing your own dirty work this time."

"Cara, you *don't* have a choice."

"Really? What are you going to do to me now? Before, you threatened to pin Paula's murder on me. Now you've framed someone else. Like you said yesterday, I'm free."

"Yeah, I know. But that was before I got the message through Sam. Tomorrow you *will* be free. And a lot richer. You can leave this town. Never have to see me again. Start fresh—anywhere you want."

I stilled. Richer?

"Think about that, Cara. Think what you could do for your daughter."

The mention of money was another manipulation, I knew that. A bread crumb trail before a starving dog. But, God forgive me, I took a bite. "What do you mean, richer?"

Something flicked across J.L.'s face. He knew he had me. I hated him for that.

"You're right." He shrugged. "Vince gets a cut of the money. And I get a part of his cut. The total is thirty thousand per shipment. Len will count it out to you. Vince expects me to keep it all this time, payment for the job. But you can have it. All of it."

Thirty thousand dollars? It was a fortune. A year's salary.

"It's so easy, Cara. You can pay off your lease, pack up and leave. All of this will be behind you."

Thirty thousand dollars. Riley and I could move clear across the country. The *life* I could build for her.

I squeezed my eyes shut. This was insane. It was drug money. Blood money. Would some of that cash be the very same bills that Blaze had paid for his heroin?

J.L. shot me a look. "I don't have to make this so easy for you, you know. I could demand my cut of the money. I could demand *all* of it. I'm being generous."

How thoughtful. "Do you really expect me to believe Vince will never hear I went instead of you? Of course he'll hear it. He may be in jail, but somehow he'll know."

"So what?" J.L. spread his hands. "He's stuck there. He's gonna be convicted for Paula's murder. Meanwhile, you're long gone. As for Len, he won't care. His shipment will go out as usual, that's all he's worried about. After tonight he'll just have to find someone else to transport the money."

I pressed a hand against my temple. Stared at the carpet. How had I gotten here? How had my life led to *this*? Murder. Drugs. This didn't happen to people. It couldn't be real.

"J.L., what you're asking me to do is impossible. First of all, Riley's at home. What am I supposed to do—leave her alone after dark?"

"She'll be asleep. She won't even know you're gone."

"Asleep?"

"I'll set the meeting for later than usual. At midnight."

"Midnight?" This man had lost his mind. "You want me to meet in the middle of the night with some drug kingpin who'd probably just as soon kill me as give me a cut of his money? Where would *that* leave my daughter?"

"That won't happen, Cara. It's in his best interest to do the transaction as he always has. He doesn't care about the thirty thousand, that's nothing to him."

"Thirty thousand is nothing? How could they possibly make so much money every six days?"

J.L. tilted his head, as if deciding whether to answer. "It's a big network. Stretches all over the state and more. They bring the money here 'cause we're an hour and a half from the Canadian border."

I studied J.L. So sure of himself. Of his power. "You're taking an awful big risk, telling me this. What's to keep me from going to the Sheriff's Office right now?"

A slow smile spread across J.L.'s face. He lifted his hand and pointed at me. "Because I know you'll do the right thing. You'll put your daughter first—and take the money."

"That's not the 'right' thing."

"Oh, but it is for you, Cara. It certainly is." J.L. snatched up my phone.

"Stop! What are you—

"What's your passcode?"

"Are you calling that man again?"

"*What* is your code?"

"I'm not telling you!"

J.L. lowered the cell. His back straightened. "Wanna rethink that, Cara?" He ground out the words. "I can *make* you tell me."

A nerve-sizzle began in my head. Spread down my body.

"Tell me. *Now.*"

No, no, no.

He took a step toward me.

I shrank away. "One-seven-two-three!"

J.L. stopped. Smiled. "*Thank* you."

He tapped in the numbers. I heard a phone ring.

"Yeah." Same man's voice.

"Hawaii. A woman's coming." J.L. kept hard eyes on me.

"A *woman*?"

"Give her Vince's cut."

"What's my assurance?"

"Her address is 1612 Grant Street. She has a teenage daughter."

My lungs shriveled.

"How old?"

"Thirteen."

A chuckle. "Nice age."

A ball lodged in my throat, swelled it shut.

J.L. ended the call.

He held the phone out to me. I couldn't move.

"Now. Cara. You will go tonight. I'll give you all the information you need. You go and do your job, and you'll be fine. No one will bother you or Riley. And she'll be safe by herself till you get back. But Len is not a guy you want to cross."

I lowered my eyes. A tear fell on my cheek.

"Understand me?"

Riley. My Riley. What I had done to her. "I thought you cared for children, J.L. Remember that?"

"Cara. *Do* you understand me?"

My head nodded.

J.L. sniffed. "Now, come on, don't be so upset. You're getting what you want, I'll bet. A way out. Soon you'll be long gone from here."

"Soon" wasn't soon enough. No way could I make plans to move a week or two from now, with that evil man, Len, knowing my address. I'd have to leave tonight. Forget my furniture. Just wake up Riley the minute I got home—and we'd be gone.

The man's sneering chuckle echoed in my head. How could J.L. do this? His own daughter was thirteen. How could he *do* this?

Sudden rage exploded inside me. I wanted Paula's scarf in my hands. I could almost feel it weave through my fingers. I'd wrap it around J.L.'s neck and yank the ends. Choke him to death. Laugh like a maniac as the life drained out of his face.

J.L. laid my phone on the desk. "I need to tell you how this'll work tonight."

My palm raised. "Not now." I couldn't stomach the sound of his voice.

"But you've got to know—"

"*Later*, J.L." I raised my eyes to his. "Haven't you said enough for the moment? I'll *do* it, okay? You got me. Through my *daughter*. So just … back off a minute."

J.L.'s gaze chilled. "Fortunately for you, I'm a patient man. Plus, you need to be thinking straight. So I'll give you half an hour." One side of his mouth twisted upward. "Tomorrow, when you're thirty thousand dollars richer—you'll thank me for this."

With a smug blink, he turned and headed for his office.

CHAPTER 41

They say your life comes down to a few pivotal moments. Those you remember as you're dying. The minutes that followed after J.L. closed his office door behind him are forever branded in my brain.

Watching me, you'd never have guessed it. I sat motionless in my desk chair, staring at the antler coat tree across the room. A symbol of J.L. My limbs had filled with meltwater, cold and deadening. But my mind whirled. Fragments of scenes and conversations, dreams and dashed hopes, gusted in my head. The noise was so loud I thought I would blow apart.

How far I'd fallen from the woman, the mother, I'd wanted to be.

I told myself I could still rebuild. Tomorrow. After this was over I would learn to be strong, stand up for myself. Grip God's great fingers with my own feeble ones and never let go. I would raise my daughter to love Him, too. Teach her what is right. With the fresh start money, I'd give her chances she and I had never experienced.

Maybe the guilt would fade in time. In the end, money is just ... money, right? It would buy our necessities, regardless of where it had come from. As for Vince Rayle—as J.L. said, he was hardly a law-abiding citizen. He'd be in prison for the wrong crime, but he did deserve to be there. And J.L., himself? Someday he'd trip up. He'd get what was coming to him. If not in this life, in the next.

Besides, what choice did I have?

When I thought I could take no more, the chaos in my head finally began to subside. Little by little, my mind cleared. Ideas, at first faint, drifted through, allowing new focus. Logic appeared, trailing details.

How could I do this?

If I went through with it, I would need inner strength such as I'd never possessed.

At some point I blinked and looked around, as if coming out of a coma. My legs felt stiff, and my back ached. I rolled the chair away from my desk and stood. Stretched. Dragged in long breaths.

I checked the wall clock. My half hour was almost up.

My cell phone lay on the desk, where J.L. had placed it. I couldn't stand the thought of his fingerprints mingling with mine. With a tissue I wiped it clean. Typed in my passcode and checked for messages from Riley that I may not have heard arrive in my fugue state.

Nothing.

The grating chuckle of that evil man echoed again in my head. I shivered. My cell could not stay within J.L.'s reach anymore. It went into my purse.

God, help me do what I have to do.

J.L.'s door opened. He approached my desk. Looked down at me, the powerful man to his peon. "I assume you're ready to talk now."

I gazed at him with defiance. "I'm ready to say how much I hate you for what you've done to me."

He gave me a patronizing smile. "Are you quite through? You need this information. It will save your life. And Riley's."

My fingers curled. "I'm listening."

For the next five minutes he told me what I needed to know. "That's it, Cara. Not hard. You got everything?"

I nodded.

"Now don't do anything stupid. Remember, you don't show up, Len knows where to find you. And Riley."

His last two words pierced. "How could I forget?"

"That's the spirit. And don't get some smart idea about telling on me, either. No one would believe you, especially my good friend the Sheriff. Even those calls to that drug dealer—they're on *your* phone."

Of course. He'd staged that, too, just like my fingerprints inside Paula's purse. "J.L. I have no proof of *anything*."

He wagged his head. "That's right, you don't. I know you don't want to be sleeping in jail tonight, leaving your daughter all alone. And with Len knowing your address."

A lightning bolt of terror shot through me. If ever I would have fallen apart, it was then. Somehow I stuck to the plan.

Clinging to the edge of my desk, I pulled to my feet. My ankles shook. "I'm going home now."

J.L. raised his eyebrows. "It's nine-fifteen."

My heart pummeled my ribs. Surely J.L. heard it. "What am I going to do here for the rest of day? Answer your phone? Pay your bills? I've got to pack. I'm leaving town tonight. You'll be rid of me. All your plans will be completed to perfection. Paula dead, Vince in jail, now this. What do you care if you lose a few hours of honest work from me?"

He regarded me coolly. Then waved his hand in the air. "Go. Just get your job done tonight."

Just like that—I was dismissed. Out of his life. The *arrogance* of the man. So sure of his total control over me, even when I was out of his sight.

I picked up my purse and made for the door. I just wanted out of there. As I grabbed the doorknob, I knew he'd stop me at the last minute. Pull me back. And all would be lost.

He said not a word.

My trembling hand yanked back the door. I stumbled out of that detestable office—into my dark future.

CHAPTER 42

I sped home to Riley, fingers curled around the steering wheel in a death grip. That horrible laugh grated in my head.

"Nice age … nice age … nice age."

Not for a minute could I allow Riley to be home alone now.

In my garage, I smacked the button to slide down the door. I jumped out of the car, Riley already appearing in the threshold to the kitchen. "How come you're home?"

She took in my expression, and her smile slipped. "What's wrong?"

"Come inside."

Taking her arm, I steered her toward the kitchen table. "Sit down. We need to talk."

She obeyed, shoulders hunched. "What did I do?"

Tears sprang to my eyes. "Nothing, honey. This isn't about you. It's *for* you. My job is over. I'm not going back."

Riley's eyes rounded. "Why?"

"I can't work for him anymore. He's … like his daughter."

Understanding played across Riley's face. "He's lying about you?"

How to answer that?

"Is he making you *do* things?" Riley's voice rose.

I rested my hand over hers. "It's okay. It doesn't matter now."

Her cheeks flushed, a sick expression creasing her face. "I hate him. Morgan, too. I hate them both!"

"I know. I know."

"I don't want to go to school with her anymore."

"You won't have to. We're leaving here."

Riley blinked. Seconds passed before she could speak. "Where are we going?"

Her voice was so small, it broke my heart. "Are you sorry?"

"No." She licked her lips. "It's just … we started over a few weeks ago, and it was supposed to be good. Now …"

"I know. This time it will be better. I promise."

"Where are we going?"

"I don't know."

"When?"

"Soon. Look, I can't tell you everything right now. I just … need you to trust me. I need you to do whatever I tell you, even if you don't understand why. In time you will. Can you do that?"

She gazed at me, fear in her eyes. "Are we in trouble?"

"Can you *do* that, Riley?"

She nodded.

"Good. Okay." I squeezed her hand and stood. We had to get moving. "Right now I need you to pack up everything you want to take with you. I'll do the same. It all needs to fit in the car."

"What about my bed and stuff?"

"We'll worry about the big things later."

She pushed back her chair and stood.

"And, Riley, turn off your phone. It's really important that we keep this secret. *No* communication with anyone. Turn it *off*."

"Okay."

I pulled her to my chest. "I love you so much. We'll get through this."

She held me tightly, then disappeared into her bedroom.

In my own room, I grabbed my computer and turned it on. Sat down on the bed and began searching for the information I needed. What I learned—it was good. *Good.*

Next—I needed to find an attorney.

I certainly couldn't go to Sam Merilen, "the best attorney in town." In fact, I didn't want any lawyer from Payton. J.L.'s power was far too strong. I started in Coeur d'Alene, bouncing from one website to another. How to choose? I had no idea. I could only beg God for guidance.

I searched until a name caught my eye. *Dede Traxton.* A woman in her … fifties, maybe? Gray-brown hair. Friendly face. She looked … nice. Capable. And I'd had enough of men.

Pulse fluttering, I picked up my phone and keyed in her number. Then sat staring at it.

This was it. My Rubicon.

The cell felt hot in my hand.

But Dede was just an attorney, not law enforcement. Client privilege would prevail, right? If I changed my mind after talking to her, she couldn't tell anyone.

My finger hovered. I'll admit it shook.

I took a deep breath—and pressed *call.*

The attorney answered on the first ring. "Dede Traxton."

My mouth opened, but nothing came out.

"Hello?"

"H-hi. I … need a lawyer."

"Here I am. What can I help you with?"

My heart pounded. I struggled to firm my voice. "I—I know about a murder. And about international money laundering for drug sellers."

"Wow. That's what I call an opening statement."

Was I really doing this? I couldn't get enough oxygen.

"You still there?" she asked.

"Yes."

"Talk to me."

"I will. And I'll tell law enforcement everything I know. On one condition. I want full immunity. And protection for me and my daughter."

CHAPTER 43

".... And protection for me and my daughter."

The final sentence poured out of me.

I sat back in my hard chair at the Sheriff's Office headquarters, spent. For hours I'd been telling my story nonstop, right up to the moment I called Dede. I'd told them everything. What had happened. What I'd felt. I wanted every person in the room to know the terror I'd been through. And to understand who I am. Why I hadn't come forward until now.

This time I was in no small interrogation room. Too many people for such cramped quarters. We sat around a rectangular table in some office, I at one end. My attorney, Dede Traxton, was on my right. Across from her were Eric Chandler and David Heldman, a drug crime investigator from the Sheriff's Office. On Dede's side of the table sat two FBI agents who'd quickly flown over from Seattle. I only remembered their first names. Charles and Tom. The Kootenai County Prosecuting Attorney, Randy Zuhle, sat at the far end of the table.

A camera had videotaped my entire statement. It still ran.

The meeting had been hastily assembled after I met with Dede in her Coeur d'Alene office. I took Riley with me to that meeting. As I talked to Dede, Riley waited in the reception area, knowing little of what was going on. She never dreamed it had anything to do with Paula Tellinger. She guessed it was about Blaze's death from heroin.

Maybe, indirectly, it was.

After Dede and I met, the attorney sprang into action, contacting the FBI regarding the money laundering, then authorities in Kootenai County. "Don't mention J.L. Larrett's name," I'd insisted to her. Who knew if I could trust the Sheriff's Office? J.L. seemed to think he had them in his pocket. I would reveal the identity of Paula's real killer when everyone was assembled and my demands had been granted.

Negotiations flew back and forth. The deal so easily could have fallen through. The Sheriff's Office already had their suspect for Paula's murder, and the evidence to convict him. It was going to take a lot to prove that was all a frame-up. But J.L.'s own statements to me gave them reason to listen. The Sheriff's Office had kept a tight lid on the evidence they had against Vince Rayle. Paula's purse stashed in his closet, wrapped in a towel with blood on it. His house key. So how would I know those details?

Now, somewhere in the building, Riley waited for me again, watched over by a female deputy. Riley still did not know what was happening. But she trusted me.

When I finished my story, the room fell silent. Shock and betrayal flattened Eric Chandler's face. I knew the feeling.

"So you have the tape?" FBI agent Charles asked.

"Yes." Dede gestured for me to pull out my phone. "Still on her cell. And I've made multiple copies."

I tapped in my passcode and started the tape, shivering at the memory of J.L.'s hands on me. If he hadn't accosted me about taping his words, I'd never have thought of it.

"I assume you're ready to talk now." J.L.'s voice filled the room.

"I'm ready to say how much I hate you for what you've done to me."

We listened as J.L. told me the address of Vince Rayle's company. The code to the digital lock that would open his warehouse. Where to find the keys to the four locked trucks inside. He made me repeat all the information until he was satisfied I remembered.

"You don't have to worry about pulling up the false floors in the trucks. Len will pack the money and secure the floors. All you have to do is unlock each truck and let him in. And get your thirty thousand dollars. When he's gone, lock each truck, put back the keys, and turn the digital dial to lock the warehouse. You gotta make it look like nobody's been in there, so the drivers who come in the next day won't suspect anything."

"They don't know?" My voice sounded so frightened.

"They have no idea. They'll pick up their product and drive it to Canada."

"But ... how does the money get out of the truck?"

"The drug people have someone on the other side. They'll reverse what you did here. The money will be run through financial institutions."

Silence. I closed my eyes, remembering that moment. How my heart had been hammering.

"Why Canada? Why not just do it here, without all the risk?"

"It's easier there. Their financial institutions—the laws are more lax."

The two FBI agents shook their heads, as if they knew that fact all too well.

We listened as J.L. warned me not to be "stupid." That no one in the Sheriff's Office would believe me if I told.

I glanced at Eric. His head was down, his focus on the table. But I saw the pain on his face.

Then came my closing speech.

"What am I going to do here for the rest of day? Answer your phone? Pay your bills? I've got to pack. I'm leaving town tonight. You'll be rid of me. All your plans will be completed to perfection. Paula dead, Vince in jail, now this. What do you care if you lose a few hours of honest work from me?"

"Go. Just get your job done tonight."

I switched off the tape.

The Prosecuting Attorney leaned back in his chair and regarded the ceiling.

I could imagine his thoughts of J.L.'s future defense arguments in court. The recording didn't contain an actual confession to the murder and framing of Vince Rayle, Dede had warned me. But with everything else, it should be enough to convict J.L.

At least I knew he couldn't be represented by his good buddy Sam Merilen. Sam was already Vince's lawyer.

I rubbed my arms. "Sorry it's not everything you'd like to hear. If I had tried to get all the details in, he may have suspected me again of taping him. If he'd demanded to see my phone ..."

Dede waved a hand in the air. "Cara, you did *great.* You got what you could at tremendous risk to yourself."

"Agreed." Eric nodded.

I shot him a grateful glance. "I didn't want to lie to you all those times. I'm so sorry. Do you *see* why I didn't tell the truth earlier? Without this tape, I'd have had no proof at all."

"I know. I get it."

"And he threatened *my daughter.* Who's the same age as his own." My voice turned strident. "That was *it* for me. *That* I could not take. He gave her up to a *drug dealer* if I didn't do what he said!"

My face crumpled. I fought for control.

"It's okay, now, Cara." Dede patted my hand. "It's okay."

"Well, it's not." I looked from the FBI agents to the Prosecuting Attorney. "Not until you convict him. For all of it. You'd better do that. You'd better get that horrible man off the streets!"

"We'll get him." Zuhle looked me in the eye. "I promise you."

FBI agent Tom folded his hands on the table. "We're grateful for all you're doing. And we'll also keep our promise to you and make sure you and your daughter are protected."

"Thank you. So much."

For right now, Riley and I would stay in a hotel. Guarded. But soon our lives would change completely. We'd be entering the federal witness protection program. That fact still hadn't sunk in. Testifying against J.L. regarding the murder of Paula Tellinger wouldn't have warranted going to such lengths. Testifying against his money laundering for an international drug ring was another matter.

What my life had come to.

"But right now you know we still need your help," Tom said. "As brave as you've been, your work's not done yet."

"I ... know."

The most terrifying task of all lay ahead.

CHAPTER 44

Eleven forty-five.

The dark streets on the outskirts of Payton were empty, save for my car. Threatening clouds hung low, covering the moon and stars. I drove stiff-spined, back not touching the seat, as I'd done six nights before on the way to dispose of Paula's body. Constant prayers ran through my mind. Thanks to Jesus for what He'd granted me so far. Protection in what I was about to do. Help for Riley and me in our future. I asked for justice. And forgiveness for all I'd done.

Rayle Trucking's warehouse sat in a light industrial area just off Highway 95. Tall poles holding security lights dotted the deserted parking area. All were dark. Just like J.L. had said.

I pulled to a stop in front of the entrance.

My palms felt clammy as I reached for the car door handle. Memories of leaving Riley in our hotel room flashed in my mind. She'd hugged me hard, crying. The female deputy with her assured that I'd be okay. By then Riley knew a little more about what was happening. "Some people committed crimes," I'd told her. "I was a witness. Now I have to help catch them."

"Do it, Mom." Riley finally drew away from me, fear and defiance creasing her face. "So we can get out of this town."

She still had no idea what *getting out of this town* would mean. How even her name would have to change.

As I slid from the car, frigid air clawed through my coat. I shivered.

The oppressive night swallowed all sound as I made my way to the digital lock on the office's entrance door. In the darkness I could barely find it. I slid my cell from my coat pocket and turned on the flash. Sudden light leapt. I peered over my shoulder, nerves tingling, but could see nothing. No one.

Still, Len could be out there somewhere. Watching me. Making sure I was alone.

I bent over the lock and started turning the dial. J.L.'s voice echoed in my brain. *Two turns right, thirty ... One turn left, eighty-five ... Immediate turn right, forty-six.*

The lock clicked. I turned off my phone's flash and slid it into my pocket. Pushed the door open. Felt around the corner to flick on an overhead light.

I slipped inside and closed the door.

Air raked over my throat as I veered left to open another door into a pitch-black warehouse. I flipped a switch, and light flooded the area.

Five high bay doors in a row, again as J.L. had told me. Four identical trucks should be lined up in front of the closest four doors, although I couldn't see all of them from where I stood. Beyond them, the fifth parking space should be empty.

My breath misted in the cold air.

On a back wall sat a gray metal cabinet. Keys to each of the trucks would be inside. A back door was next to the cabinet.

Before entering the warehouse, I followed J.L.'s directive and turned off the light in the office.

I stepped into the warehouse, closing the door behind me. On the wall next to the light switch sat control buttons for the bay doors, marked one through five.

My gaze slid over the nearest truck. A man could so easily hide behind it, or any one of the others.

"What if Len is already there?" I'd asked the FBI agents.

"If he could get inside, he wouldn't need you. And we'll be watching the place. Plus, we'll be right there."

They didn't know who Len was. And the tape I'd given them held only J.L.'s word. Len had to be lured to the place and caught in the act of doing what J.L. had said he would: stashing money under the fake floor in one of the trucks. With that airtight evidence, law enforcement could lean on him to give up the people above himself in the drug trade. And as soon as they had Len in custody, J.L. would be arrested at his house.

More than once I'd pictured the middle-of-the-night pounding on J.L.'s door. Him being taken away in pajamas and handcuffs.

My pulse stumbled, leaving me light-headed. I forced my feet down the length of the closest truck, toward the back of the warehouse. Feeling watchful eyes follow me. Wherever the cameras were, the FBI agents had hidden them well.

I rounded the corner to cross in front of the first truck. The other three came into view. As I passed the first, and the second, I gazed down the long spaces in between them.

No one.

After an eternity I reached the cabinet. The door squeaked as it opened. Four keys hung on hooks on the right side. I took them out.

My watch read eleven fifty-five. Only minutes to go. I needed to move faster.

I unlocked the warehouse's back door. That, J.L. had not told me to do.

One by one I hurried to the rear of each truck and opened their loading doors, leaving the keys dangling from their locks. Fear gripped me tighter with every move. By the time I finished, my ankles wobbled, and my lungs screamed for air.

I scurried back toward the office, pulling in deep breaths.

"*Turn out the warehouse lights,*" J.L. had said. "*Then open bay door five. Len will pull his truck inside. Let the door close completely before you turn the light back on.*"

I reached the bay door buttons and lay my finger over number five.

Muscles deep inside me fluttered. This was it. If anything went wrong, it would be now.

With my other hand, I turned off the lights.

The warehouse plunged into blackness. I could hear my own breathing.

I pressed button five. The farthest bay door began to open.

My heart ricocheted around my ribs. I leaned against the wall and listened to the gears grind. I did not take my left finger off button five.

The door stopped.

Silence.

Air sputtered in and out of my mouth. I strained to hear the sound of an approaching truck.

Nothing.

How long would I have to wait? What if Len never came? What if he'd found out somehow?

What if he *did* come? I'd have to face him. Likely endure his pat-down, looking for a wire. Yes, law enforcement men crouched behind the building, listening for their cue from those watching the video feed. Still, it would only take an instant—

Rumbling in the distance. An engine.

The noise grew louder. Then a pause, as if the vehicle was turning into the parking lot.

Lights swung through the open bay door.

A truck chugged closer, then appeared. It rolled through the bay door and stopped. The engine shut off. The lights cut. Blackness fell over the warehouse once again.

I pressed the button, and the door began to close.

I huddled in the darkness, *feeling* the evilness of the man in the truck. The one who liked girls the age of my daughter.

Sudden quiet. I flipped the switch—and the warehouse flooded with light. I blinked in the brightness.

What next, what next? I couldn't remember. Was I supposed to go to him? Or he to me?

Nothing moved.

I eased away from the wall. Edged toward the back of the warehouse. My head floated, my feet a mile away. I rounded the front of the first truck, and the new one in bay five came into view. Len sat in the driver's seat. I couldn't see his face. He motioned for me to keep coming.

How could I allow myself to be alone with this man?

Why had I done this? Riley and I could be hundreds of miles away by now. With no money, and likely chased for what I knew, but I wouldn't be *here*. A walking target to be taken out with one easy shot.

My legs took me past the second and third trucks. Len opened his door and got out of the vehicle. He made no further move. Just waited, his back to me.

Not until I edged around the front of his truck did he look familiar.

J.L. turned around.

I stilled. The heat of the truck's engine wafted around me. "Why are you here?"

"Change of plans. Len's not available tonight."

I stared at him. What was going on? "Why didn't you call me? You could have gotten in by yourself."

A slow smile spread across J.L.'s face. "No harm in seeing you one more time. Nice to see you're still doing what you're told. Not that I expected any less."

I thought of Riley. Safe in our hotel room.

J.L. gestured with his chin. "You got all the trucks unlocked?"

"Yes."

"Let's pack up, then. You can help." He swiveled and started toward the rear of the vehicle, light in his step. So sure of himself— and wanting me to know it.

I couldn't move. None of this felt right, but my brain couldn't process.

"Come on, Cara." He opened the back of his truck. Something thudded onto the warehouse floor. "Start carrying these over to be loaded."

I inched around the opened doors to see long cellophane-wrapped packages of bills on the floor. Even though I'd expected this, the sight still took my breath away. So much money! From inside the truck, J.L. tossed more out. "These are packed to fit perfectly under the flooring." He threw one close to my feet. "Four feet long and eleven inches high."

Why hadn't Len come? Now the FBI couldn't catch him, couldn't stop the drug trade. Would they go back on their word to protect me and Riley?

"Bet you've never seen so much money all in one place before." J.L. laughed.

"N-no."

"Come on, get moving and help me."

My mind clicked into focus. Maybe they could still catch Len— through J.L. I had to play my part. *Cara, you can do this.* "Show me how to open up the flooring. I'll start putting these inside."

J.L. smirked. "That's more like it."

"I just want to get home to my daughter."

"Sure you do." He jumped out of the truck. "Come on."

I lifted a package and followed.

At the next truck over, J.L. flung open the rear doors. He climbed inside and shuffled, bent-backed, to the very front. Then turned around to stoop down, feeling the dusty floor just in front of himself at the corner. He pushed—and one long half of the floor before him popped open. He moved to the other side and pushed. The other half opened. He pulled up both doors until they pointed at the truck's ceiling.

"See? Clever, huh."

"Yeah."

"Know what else is clever?"

That smirk again. So snide.

"What?"

"There *is* no Len. Never was."

I gazed at him blankly.

J.L. stepped down onto the hidden floor and walked toward me, no longer needing to bend over. He stopped at the edge of the truck. "*There is no Len.* I'm Len." His hateful mouth curved.

Huh?

"But … but I heard him on the phone. You talked to him. Twice. He said terrible things—"

The words cut short. Yes. He'd said awful things. About Riley.

"You paid someone to say that? To terrify me? To get me here tonight?"

J.L. lifted a shoulder. "A druggie'll do anything for money. Come tomorrow, he won't even remember."

But why? *Why* did J.L. want me here?

The smile disappeared from his face. He jumped out of the truck. "It's over, Cara."

He yanked a gun from his pocket.

"Get on your knees."

The world blurred. "I … what …?"

"Get down." Steel coated his words. "And put your hands on your head."

"Wh-why?"

"Cara. It's done."

No, no, no. It couldn't end like this. Pleas spilled out of me. "You don't want to give me the money, fine, just let me go."

"I am letting you go. Your body's gonna take a ride under that floor, across the Canadian border. Surrounded by money. Little surprise for the men on the other side. But who are they going to tell?" J.L. laughed. "No one will ever find you. They'll never know what happened to you."

Riley. "No! Please! I won't tell anybody about any of this."

"That's the plan."

"You can't *do* this! You can't take me away from my daughter."

J.L. made a disgusted sound in his throat. "What good are you to your daughter? *Look* at yourself."

"J.L., you're a father. *Please.* I *have* to get back to her!"

"She's better off without you. Tell you what, I'll raise her myself."

My brain exploded.

Adrenaline flooded every vein. My foot kicked up, hard. Hit J.L. in the groin. He gasped, stumbled back. I swung a fist at his hand. It jerked upward. His gun fired at the ceiling.

Feet pounded. Men shouted.

"Drop the weapon!"

"Drop the gun!"

"Cara, get back!"

J.L. doubled over, cheeks red and puffing for air.

I kicked him again.

He groaned and fell to his knees. The gun clattered from his hand. I sent it spinning with a foot.

"Cara, get away!"

FBI agents and Sheriff's deputies closed in, guns pointed down at J.L. "On your stomach. Now!"

Someone grabbed my elbow. Pulled me backward.

"Nnno!" I flailed and screeched, a raging wild woman. J.L. Larrett had ruined my life. Tried to kill me, take me away from my daughter. *No one* could stop me now. I wrenched from the agent's grasp and threw myself on top of J.L. My fists pummeled his back, his head, screams flying from my mouth. Strong hands grasped me, wrapped around my limbs, and still I punched and yelled and pounded until two men picked me up by the limbs like some seizuring puppet.

"Stop! Cara!"

"You could've got yourself killed!"

They carried me some distance and laid me on the cold cement floor.

"Stay here now. Shh, shh, it's okay."

It wasn't okay. My head buzzed. Dizziness whirled between my eyes.

Far away I heard more commands barked at J.L. His groans, the click of handcuffs.

"Do you have him?" My voice shook.

"We have him."

"*Do* you *have* him?"

"We got him, Cara. It's good. You did it."

I slapped away their arms. Pushed myself to sit up. I raked a long look over J.L.'s body. Saw him face down, hands cuffed behind him. Trapped. Helpless. Just like he'd made me feel.

"Don't let him go, hear me? Don't *ever* ... let him ..."

Dark spots scuttled across my vision. I couldn't blink them away. Nausea roiled. My jaw dropped open to drag in air ... but not enough.

Never enough.

"She's fainting." A man's voice.

I sagged to one side.

"Hold onto her."

Still I struggled. I didn't want to miss any of it. Wanted to see them take J.L. away. Toss him in prison. Throw away the key. But sight and sound faded. And I just ....

Couldn't ....

"Don't ever ..." I gasped. "Let him ...."

The world crashed.

ONE YEAR LATER

EPILOGUE

Thanksgiving Day.

Our little house in Memphis, Tennessee fills with the enticing smells of baking turkey and stuffing. Gravy is just beginning to bubble on the stove. My daughter, Annie, hums under her breath as she sets the table for three.

Annie. It took a lot of practice to stop calling her Riley. Her full name now is Annette Nicole McKnight. She came up with it herself. Mine is Krista Mae McKnight. Again—from my daughter's creativity.

"What time is Ben coming over?" She drops a fork, and it clatters against a plate. "Oops, sorry."

"Soon."

On cue a knock sounds at the front door. Annie goes to pull back the bolt. "Hi! Happy Thanksgiving!" Her voice filters into the kitchen.

"You, too, Annie Boo." Ben speaks with a Southern drawl.

"Oh, no, he's talking in rhymes again." Annie laughs.

"You know you love it."

I walk around the corner into the living room. Ben is giving Annie a hug.

Warmth fills me as I watch them. He's a loving Christian man, and quite the tease. The kind of man Annie should have had for a father.

Maybe someday he'll be her stepfather. I hope so. It's surprising that I'm thinking in those terms already. I don't have the easiest time trusting men. And I only met him six months ago, just after my nerve-wrenching days on the stand in Idaho, testifying in J.L.'s trial. But Annie loves Ben already, as I do.

We are both so ready to be loved.

Ben lets Annie go and walks over to me. "Lovely Krista." He gives me a kiss.

"Where's *her* rhyme?" Annie wants to know.

"On her finga there's a blista."

My daughter and I groan.

"Come on into the kitchen." I take Ben's hand. "Dinner's almost ready."

"Good, I'm starved. Can I help?"

"Nope, just sit."

We chat about our jobs as Annie and I put dinner on the table. When the Witness Protection Program moved Annie and me to Memphis, they helped me find employment as an admin for an insurance company. Ben, an attorney in business law, has an office in the same building—which is how we met. The fact that he's an attorney thrills Annie. She no longer wants to be a baker when she grows up. Not after what we've been through. Now her future plans are all about becoming a lawyer.

Ben does not know our real names or our story. It's a sad and ironic fact that we have to hide that truth from him. From everyone.

Only if he asks me to be his wife will I tell him. He would deserve to know. And he'd need to understand why the past so haunts me. My days in court were some of my hardest. Just seeing J.L. again, having to face him in person, shook me to the core. By then, of course, the investigation into all his crimes was complete. Through Dede I learned details I had not known before. Every one of them proved my statements true. Details such as a dog trained to sniff human remains hitting on the trunk of Paula's car. Hair from her, and a chip of fingernail polish inside that trunk. A blonde hair on the driver's seat matched to me. Security camera footage of J.L.'s SUV taking a roundabout route to meet me on Shelkins Road that night of the murder. Another camera capturing his car near Vince Rayle's house as he drove to plant the evidence. A third camera catching him on Highway 95 as he drove back to the forest to drop the key.

And J.L. had thought himself so clever.

Apparently the only truth J.L. had told was that, after four years of laundering money for drug dealers, he'd wanted out. But that's not something you just stop doing. My guess is that, when his office assistant, Edith, suddenly died, J.L. saw his chance and began laying his plans. Hire someone like me ... kill Paula ... frame Vince ... kill me.

Only a man full of himself would think he could get away with that.

Vince Rayle testified against J.L., too. Wish I could have seen it. Dede told me how it went. Vince, the friend and client betrayed, held nothing back, including his contempt for the defendant. J.L. had known him all too well—enough to predict that he would lie regarding his whereabouts the night Paula went missing. Vince couldn't exactly tell law enforcement he'd been helping J.L. load drug money into his trucks late that night. And he figured it was better to claim he'd been at his Priest River house from early evening on than to leave any hours open in Payton, during which time he could have done something to his ex.

Vince's sentence was reduced in exchange for his testimony.

J.L. was another story. The night of his arrest he was offered a plea deal for the money laundering charge in return for giving up the names of the drug sellers. He refused. He did not believe he could be protected against retaliation in jail. Someone would shank him for certain. And he was even more frightened for his wife and daughter. An offer to place them in witness protection hadn't swayed him. The offer was taken off the table when law enforcement caught the drug dealers another way. Officers were waiting in Canada when men came to the trucks, expecting to unpack the cash. Those men rolled over on the drug traders above them.

By the time of J.L.'s trial, his house was up for sale, and his wife and daughter had moved back East to live near Rachelle's parents. J.L. was convicted of all charges and received life in prison with no parole.

Sometimes I wonder how Morgan and Rachelle are doing. How Morgan fits in at her new school, where she is a nobody. The daughter of a murderer.

I place the platter of turkey on the table, then check to make sure I've remembered everything.

"Wait, Mom, there's bread in the oven." Annie pulls it out and brings it over.

"Okay." I smile at Ben. "That's everything. Let's eat!"

Annie and I sit down. The three of us hold hands to pray.

Ben fills his plate. At the first bite of stuffing, his eyebrows rise. "Man, this is so good."

I smile at him. *Life* is becoming good. How amazing I can say that. I thought I'd plummeted too far for God to reach me. But Jesus has a very long arm.

Annie and I have not escaped without scars. She knows she can never contact anyone from her past again. Our door is always locked. Sometimes at night I lie awake, reliving all that happened. Thinking how close J.L. came to killing me. I cry and shake. Sometimes Annie wakes at night, and I go to comfort her. But Jesus, the Great Healer, is at work in our lives. We are learning how to be strong. Annie is proud of me for making the very difficult decision to tell my story one year ago. And for testifying against J.L. I am proud of her for how she is maturing. Recently she stood up against the bullying of a helpless girl in her school. She is now that girl's hero and friend.

Ben's plate is almost clean. The man eats so fast. I shake my head in wonder.

"Have some more." Annie hands him the turkey platter.

"Ah, somebody raised you right, Miss Annie McKnight."

My daughter and I exchange a smile.

Visit Brandilyn's website to read the first chapters of all her books.
www.brandilyncollins.com

On Facebook, Brandilyn can be found at:
www.facebook.com/brandilyncollinsseatbeltsuspense